DRYAD SOULED

DRYAD SOULED
DRAGON OF SHADOW AND AIR BOOK SIX

JESS MOUNTIFIELD

THE DRYAD SOULED TEAM

Thanks to our JIT Team:

Dave Hicks
Deb Mader
Veronica Stephan-Miller
Diane L. Smith
Dorothy Lloyd
John Ashmore
Thomas Ogden

If We've missed anyone, please let us know!

Editor
SkyHunter Editing Team

This book is a work of fiction. All of the characters, organizations, and events portrayed in this novel are either products of the author's imagination or are used fictitiously. Sometimes both.

Copyright © 2021 Jess Mountifield

LMBPN Publishing supports the right to free expression and the value of copyright. The purpose of copyright is to encourage writers and artists to produce the creative works that enrich our culture.

The distribution of this book without permission is a theft of the author's intellectual property. If you would like permission to use material from the book (other than for review purposes), please contact support@lmbpn.com. Thank you for your support of the author's rights.

LMBPN Publishing
PMB 196, 2540 South Maryland Pkwy
Las Vegas, NV 89109

Version 1.01 December 2021
eBook ISBN: 978-1-64971-945-4
Print ISBN: 978-1-64971-946-1

Dedication:

To the friends who are there no matter what. The ones who have your back and help you fly.

CHAPTER ONE

Two hundred and thirty-four. That was how many bricks I'd counted on the opposite wall of my cell. I'd been in it with no one but Sen for company for what felt like days.

Zephyr was in a large canopied area in a yard nearby. He could fly away if he wanted to, the only one of the three of us who could. Of course, Sen and I could have left as well if we'd truly wanted to, but that was against the point of us being here.

We were in solitary confinement in a maximum-security area of the prison. It wasn't ideal, but I had accepted it. Given what people said about female prisons, I had it fairly easy. No one was going to mess with me when they were aware my powers still worked just fine.

It was almost crazy having the guards treat me with so much more respect than everyone else around here, but there wasn't much I dared to do. I'd seen our lawyer just once.

At first, the guards had woken me up every few hours

to stop me from sleeping, but Sen and Zephyr had both turned aggressive, the dragon threatening to tear the next guard who tried it limb from limb, and Sen rushing at anyone who got too close to her tiny frame. She could move faster than most rodents, and she had spores she could release.

Of course, they didn't know for sure that Zephyr and I could communicate and tried it again an hour or so later. They came close to the door, but Zephyr had let out a loud roar and broke the chain they'd pinned him down with before shattering the nearest door to him with a single flick of his tail. On top of that, Sen chose that moment to leap up to our cell door, open the slot they used to pass me things like food, and eject a cloud of red spores through it.

As I recalled the surprise on the guard's face, I smiled. At least I wasn't in prison alone.

You should sleep. We have a big day tomorrow, Zephyr suggested.

Surely it's today already? I replied. Sen nuzzled my neck, her feet in a small cup on the pillow beside me. There wasn't much water in it—the guards were being stingy in that regard—but it would keep her alive.

Technically, yes. About four more hours until we're officially supposed to wake up. We should sleep before then.

I know.

I looked at the bricks again, beginning to count. Maybe this time, I'd fall asleep before I was done.

At some point I must have drifted off, losing count, then coming to and trying to continue later. Zephyr was asleep this time, and a slight movement of my head confirmed Sen was as well.

It felt strange when they were both asleep and I wasn't. I was so used to being connected to both of them that my mind was too quiet when they weren't sharing it with me.

I could listen in to their dreams, but I had to concentrate, and they were hard to follow even if I did. Zephyr's dreams didn't make much sense and Sen's were even worse, the myconid thinking almost entirely in pictures and color.

I wondered what Zephyr made of mine, but I never remembered to ask if he even listened in to any.

Sighing, I tried to go back to sleep again, but the truth was, I was terrified. I might have walked into the prison of my own free will, and I was convinced I was innocent of anything but defending myself. However, I was still about to be put on trial for terrorism and the murder of members of the United States Army and agents of the division of the government responsible for monitoring mythicals.

The lawyer the organization had hired for me had been able to visit me once and would be present, but he'd informed me that it would be a closed-door affair with a secret jury. There was no way to know what was coming and no way to know if the trial would be fair or not.

A part of me truly hoped it would be impartial and I would walk free in a few days or however long it took. But part of me was resigned to this being a joke. To needing something more to get the jury to believe I was innocent.

My lawyer had made sure I understood the importance of stating how I'd given myself up willingly and that I was capable of leaving the prison they were holding me in at any point. There was nowhere on the planet where I would be trapped or not able to escape. Not when I had funky elf superpowers and a dragon and a myconid to help me.

Since I was being charged with terrorism, I couldn't call anyone, and I didn't get the usual treatment. They could hold me indefinitely, and they could rig everything.

Somehow I had to find a way to melt their hearts no matter who they were, but I would be the first to admit that being able to call someone would have been helpful. Not only did I want to reassure my parents that I was okay, but I also wanted to talk to Minsheng, Daisy, and the others back at the warehouse.

I'd considered bringing my communication stone in with me so I could talk to Ronan, the centaur who helped guard the warehouse sometimes, but I knew he was going to be grieving his friend and mentor, Lorcan. I also didn't think the people here were going to take too kindly to me entering a trance with a stone on my forehead.

There was also the safety of the stone to consider. I'd promised Ronan and Lorcan I'd keep it a secret. I didn't want the guards to try to take it because they saw me using it and didn't understand.

Humans could sometimes activate them if they had some mythical DNA in their family tree. I couldn't take the risk one of the guards might have what they needed, so it was back in my room, along with the pot plant I'd been caring for and several of my most prized possessions.

There were two exceptions: my bracers and my necklace. I could take neither off. The guards had tried their damnedest to take them from me, but they were magically fixed to me. I was pretty sure I'd taken off the necklace I'd inherited from Tuviel a couple of times, but it was as if they knew I needed them now.

It had caused some problems with the officers on the way in. They'd insisted on getting wire cutters. They'd realized I wasn't faking it when the cutters had shattered, and I'd had to use my powers to stop the flying pieces and save everyone nearby from serious wounds.

Just another thing on the list of unconventionality when it came to putting me in prison.

The sounds of footsteps on the linoleum outside my room made me finally stir enough to wake Sen.

When I heard the jangle of keys outside my door, I reached for Zephyr with my mind.

Wake up, buddy, I said. *It's showtime.*

You need to shower first, he replied, sounding only partially awake. *I've got half an hour more.*

I frowned, but he was right. There was no way I was going to turn down a shower. I couldn't get one as regularly as I'd have liked as it was.

Will we let them keep us here if we're convicted? I asked him a moment later, trying to imagine what life might be like if we were in prison a long time and not just while awaiting the trial.

Of course, some people waited weeks and even months for their trials, and I'd only been in prison a few days. Still, it was something to consider. What would it be like to be here more permanently?

We'll take ourselves somewhere else. Promise to be good boys and girls if we can live on an island by ourselves or something. But it's not going to happen. We can prove we were attacked for defending ourselves every time. Or had probable cause, or whatever Robert said.

I nodded, grateful for the vote of confidence, and let myself be led to the shower.

"Now, none of your shenanigans. Just shower quickly and get your clothes back on," the guard said.

I wasn't sure what he meant, but I didn't reply. I'd barely used my powers in prison. Only a couple of times when either another inmate had gotten a bit too friendly or the guards hadn't given me the courtesy of privacy while showering.

Again, it had served to make me grateful I had powers and wasn't actually at the mercy of anyone.

As soon as I was dressed and presentable again, Sen and I were led to a car. Not long later, Zephyr came walking around the side of the building.

They're expecting me to fly again, he said when he saw the small car.

'Fraid so, I replied, walking up to him despite the guards calling for me to get in.

I leaned my head against his, having missed his presence beside me. Normally they let us hang out together, but each night, we had to sleep separately. It felt wrong after always being with him.

It won't be much longer, he replied, having read those thoughts. *A few more days for this case, and then we'll be cleared and back to our warehouse.*

The surety in his voice almost convinced me he had no doubts, but neither of us could hide our emotions, and I could feel his anxiety. I placed a hand on his shoulder, enjoying the feel of his shiny and smooth bronze scales.

The guards had given up trying to get me into the car, but I noticed one of them had a taser out as if he'd been considering sneaking up on Zephyr or me.

"I wouldn't use that on either of us if I were you," I warned. "It bounces off the dragon's scales and starts fires."

"What about you? I'm pretty sure you're not made of anything but flesh and blood."

"I'm not," I replied. "But if you use that thing on me, my reflexes will kick in. I'll suck the air out of your lungs and the lungs of everyone within twenty feet. You'll suffocate before either of us can stop it."

It was a lie. I had no idea what would happen if I was hit with that thing, but I kept my eyes on the guard, and he faltered.

"Right," I said, snapping my head back to the guard holding the car door open. "Shall we?"

No one argued or tried anything as I got in the car. Sen dropped onto the seat beside me again, then climbed up to the window, enjoying looking out.

We were driven a long way, the cops having to stop a couple of times to use the restroom. The sun came up as we traveled, the new day bringing with it the hope we all felt that this was the beginning of the end.

They were estimating that it would take three days for the court to hear everything, and then they were due to decide as swiftly as possible, the jury being kept locked in a room until they'd made their minds up.

When our car pulled up outside the courthouse, plenty of reporters were present, many with flashing cameras. I didn't see our lawyer yet, but everyone got out of my way, and Zephyr landed beside me a moment later. We'd already been briefed that he could fit inside the building with me, and it had been agreed that I was going to be taken in through the civilian entrance because of it.

That meant I could see Minsheng, Daisy, Chris, and Erlan, who were waiting just inside the building. I noticed Erlan had on a jacket with particularly large pockets, and Newton's head peeped up out of one briefly. It made me grin and wish I could see some of the others, but the obvious mythicals and anyone who might also be arrested had stayed away for safety.

They wouldn't be allowed in the courtroom, but I hugged each one of them, refusing to be rushed by the guards. Sen jumped from shoulder to shoulder, hugging everyone and grinning with pleasure, her little mushroom head wiggling back and forth when Minsheng tried to tickle her.

As Chris hugged me, I felt his fingers slip something down the top of a bracer. I had no way to know what it was, but I suspected I had a bug on me and my friends now had a way to listen in on everything.

He winked, and I gave him a knowing grin.

Did Chris just slip you something? Zephyr asked.

Yup. A bug, I think.

Useful. Shame it wasn't pizza.

I can ask for some later at the hotel.

Don't think we'll get it. It's not like we're here for a vacation.

No, but we can stay up and watch old movies all night. I think we've got a room on the top floor so you can fly in.

Do you think they go to this effort for other people who might be criminals? Zephyr asked as we walked down familiar halls into a different room than the one they'd used during the investigation. This one was smaller and set up more like an official courtroom, although a portion of the chairs near the door had been removed.

Robert was waiting inside the room, a smile on his face when he saw me, Sen, and then Zephyr as the dragon squeezed his large frame through the door to try to rest in the space that had been cleared.

The rest of the building was empty today. Zephyr's back half spilled out into the hallway, and several guards stayed out there to make sure no one came along.

The trial was supposed to be a closed-room affair. No media and no outside observers. Just the lawyers, the charged, the judge, the jury, and the guards necessary to make everyone feel safe.

I smiled as I thought about the last part. It was just a show to make them all feel better. I'd easily taken on so many men before, and few of them were even openly carrying weapons. If I'd wanted to murder them, none of them would have stood a chance, and I hoped that would work in my favor.

It took a little while for everyone else to appear, few of them wanting to go past Zephyr. Not until one jury member had stepped over his tail were the others willing to follow.

I fought to hide my grin at the whole thing, and I even caught my lawyer smirking.

They really think I'm going to eat them, don't they? Zephyr said a moment later.

Yeah. Maybe I can use it as leverage to get pizza.
Oh. In that case, I'll look a little more threatening."

I snorted before realizing no one else could hear what he was saying, then coughed into my hand.

"Can I get some water?" I asked, trying to sound as if I had a tickle in my throat. Robert gave me a look that made it clear he was curious, but he didn't do anything but hand me a bottle.

With everyone else in the room, the judge finally appeared, and we were all instructed to be seated.

CHAPTER TWO

I waited as the jury was told what I was being accused of, then it was my turn to make a statement. I had it written down, something Robert had prepared with me earlier.

"Thank you," I said as I got to my feet. "I understand this has all been a little different from normal proceedings, and I appreciate you accommodating us, especially regarding the bond between Zephyr, Sen, and me."

"Yes, well, it is what it is. Let us hear what you have to say for yourself," the judge said, sounding almost bored and more than a little grumpy.

I gulped, hoping it wasn't a sign of things to come and glanced at the papers in front of me.

"I'm Aella-Faye Carter," I said. "I grew up not far from here, adopted by two very amazing people. I believed I was human for most of my life, so I appeared human and formed friendships with humans. Then one day, I was mugged. That mugger led me to a warehouse, where I found Zephyr, the dragon you see before you. Since that night, I have been hunted, harassed, attacked, and even had snipers attempt to assassinate me."

I looked at the jury, pausing where Robert had put a marker. I couldn't read all of the people in the jury area and what they thought of me, but they were riveted if nothing else.

"In those first few months, Zephyr was tiny. He was no bigger than a cat when he hatched, but we bonded right away. The magic of the bond made me aware of him and connected and made him aware of me. At the same time, I realized I could control the air around me. I ran into a man who had studied mythicals. He took me in, taught me to control the magic I had suddenly developed, and kept me safe."

"This is all very well, but you're on trial for the murder of five government agents and soldiers and an unprovoked attack on a United States military base. This is irrelevant. What do you have to say for yourself on that score?" the judge demanded.

"I feel this leads to that and explains my reactions and beliefs, Your Honor," I replied before glancing at my notes.

The judge frowned. I thought he would stop me, but he sighed and looked down.

"Despite thinking I was safe, the agents never gave up chasing me. I spent months trying to find a mythical haven known as the Sanctuary. A peaceful group of mythicals who had hidden from the world to live in peace and happiness. I even had to leave there to avoid bringing trouble to their door. I'm sure you all know what happened next. I went public, offering those agents a chance to end things peacefully. They've continued to hound me."

Don't forget us, Zephyr said.

"They've also continued to hunt Zephyr and treat him like a threat."

"He'll be able to speak for himself in a short while," Robert said, interrupting me. "He's been accepted as a witness."

"He has?" the judge asked, his voice growing shrill. "When did a beast get given the right to talk in a court of law? We—"

"When I proved I was sentient, Your Honor," Zephyr interjected, lifting his head and taking up a little more space than he usually would. He emphasized the last two words, reminding the judge that he was supposed to be acting with dignity and grace. "I have spoken to people on many occasions and am entirely capable of rational thought. I assure you I can give an account of my own events."

I caught a grin from someone on the jury. The young man was sitting back, one arm over the back of the long bench. He looked more relaxed than everyone else put together.

"Anyway, as I was saying before I was interrupted," I said, "a mythical appeared the night before we attacked the military base. He told us his kind had been attacked and only he had managed to escape. He led me and a small team of mythicals, including Zephyr, Sen, and a centaur called Lorcan who was one of the Sanctuary's council members, to the base. We tried to subdue the forces there without lethal force. There was a mishap and a couple of guards were injured, but our medic and theirs worked together. We then liberated twelve elves who had been held there against their will and experimented on, all of whom are now at the Sanctuary, recovering from their ordeal and properly learning how to control their powers. Both Lorcan and the mythical who'd led us there lost their lives to this endeavor."

As I finished speaking, I pictured Lorcan lying on the floor of the compound, Dyneira at his side, the majestic mythical dead but still somehow managing to look peaceful.

A woman from a table on the other side of the judge swept to her feet and motioned for a TV to be turned on.

She showed footage from the night of the compound attack. It clearly depicted the events I'd referred to when the guard tower had been caught in a ball of flames.

"More than a mishap," she said. "You blew up the guard tower."

I took a deep breath while thinking about the best reply.

"I mentioned that," I said. "It was an accident. One of the elves elsewhere didn't realize the vapor cloud from Zephyr's breath was too close. When he could first breathe the vapor, it wasn't flammable. It now appears to be. I'd known for a little while, and I'd thought everyone I took into the battle was also aware."

"So, you admit that you knew this was possible."

"Of course—"

"Yet you didn't take precautions?"

"I took all the precautions I'd thought of, and I spent the next ten minutes using all the power available to me to get those men out of the fire and get them medical treatment."

"But they died."

"So I've been told, although my medical team informed me they were stable and would live before we left." I frowned, feeling flustered.

I reached out, and Zephyr sent calm feelings my way. It was enough to help me refocus. I couldn't let this woman get under my skin. She wanted that. Wanted me to say something that made me look bad.

I had to defend my position and restate what had happened again and again. I stuck to my story, but even I could see that her view of things was making me look bad, and at least a few members of the jury were beginning to look angry.

I tried not to worry about it, knowing Robert would be asking me more questions at the end to make it easier for me to convince people I was innocent of anything but defending the mythicals who had been imprisoned.

"But the crux of this is that you feel you are above the law, don't you, Aella?" the woman asked after trying for a while to get me to admit that I didn't care if people died as long as they weren't my people.

"No. If I felt that way, I wouldn't be here right now."

"You've finally been arrested. That's why you're here, but—"

"No," I interrupted. "An arrest warrant was issued for me, yes, but you could send the Army of the United States to face Zephyr, Sen, and me, and you wouldn't be able to arrest me if I wasn't willing to come and stand before you. I can hide from every method known to man to find me: heat sensors, cameras. You name it. We can fly. I could go anywhere."

The lawyer scoffed and I frowned, knowing most of

them didn't believe me. I considered showing them, making a twister right in the middle of the courtroom, or something else that would show them that I knew what I was doing, but I saw Robert shake his head as if he read my mind.

"I'm here because I want justice. I want mythicals to be free. To be treated like real people. Not hunted, or tested, or used as lab rats. I'm here because I still believe in the American justice system."

"Yes, well, it's not your beliefs on trial. It's your actions, and you killed people in cold blood because they were human."

"Objection, testifying," Robert said as he stood up.

"Please ask questions," the judge said, looking at the lawyer opposite me. She nodded before calming down.

"Do you like humans?" she asked.

"If you mean the species in general. It's not perfect, but I like many of them and humanity in general, yes."

"But you don't like all humans?"

"No, no one does. I don't like all elves, either."

"You don't?" she asked, sounding as if she didn't believe me.

"There's an elf who accused me of a bunch of stuff when I arrived at the Sanctuary because they saw me as an outsider. I grew up in the human world. I wasn't one of them."

"But you've proved you're one of them now, haven't you? Made it clear you couldn't care less about the race that raised you?"

I sighed as I shook my head. "No. I still don't get along very well with said elf. He wishes he was bonded with the last dragon left alive. But I didn't have to prove myself to him or anyone else. I've defended mythicals the way I wish someone was there to defend Zephyr and me in our earliest days, and I'll continue to do so."

"Not if you're behind bars, you won't."

I fought not to roll my eyes. I would not be behind bars, but I was beginning to feel like they were going to find me guilty and try to make it happen.

Thankfully, she soon finished her questioning, and I was allowed to take questions from my lawyer. He had me go back over several things again, asking me questions in different ways and getting me to elaborate on things I'd said earlier.

It calmed me, but the jury didn't look convinced. One woman had her arms crossed and was glaring at me. Mister Chill still appeared that way.

We went through the motions, and then I was done. Zephyr was called next, although he didn't move. He projected his voice well enough that everyone could hear him, and I was proud.

The dragon had everyone mesmerized, and I thought I saw a hint of fear as the lawyer acting for the prosecution came forward to ask him questions. Her hands shook, although she hid it by putting them on the table in front of her and leaning forward.

Zephyr's answers came thick and fast, the great dragon remaining calm under the barrage. I once again marveled at the wisdom he displayed, but again, she insinuated that he couldn't care about humans.

"On the contrary," he replied. "My genetic memories include many humans. My greatest ancestor Azargad has many memories of him and his bonded elf Tuviel working with the humans of the era to protect this planet from another threat. I have a lot of respect for the humans in my memories. There was once no difference between our kinds. We all lived together on this planet."

"What changed?" she asked.

Zephyr tipped his head to the side. It was a great question. What had led to humanity and mythicals becoming so estranged from each other?

"Many things. A religious sect played a big part. They decided our magic must be of the devil. Many elves were burned as witches. Greed played another part. Unicorns were almost wiped out for their horns in much the same way many other creatures have been hunted since. Sometimes people fear what they do not understand. People fear me, and I am constantly judged to be a beast despite everything I know."

This stunned the room into silence, and even the lawyer who was trying to get Zephyr to trip himself up didn't seem to know what to say at first.

"So you don't hate humans from thousands of years ago, but you hate us now because of what we've grown into?" she suddenly asked.

I almost shot out of my seat to object, but Robert kept me from doing so. I reached for Zephyr with my mind instead, but he was already opening his mouth to reply.

"I don't hate anyone, but there are some humans who have come to fear and hate us because we've not been in their world for too long. It's time that changed."

It didn't answer her question, but it was the best response I could have expected anyone to come up with.

I thought the questions would end there and we'd be allowed to move on, but she kept bombarding Zephyr with questions, and the clock reached five before she was done.

"Time to stop for now," Robert said. "You'll be escorted to your hotel, and you'll need to stay there and not communicate with anyone."

I nodded without thinking. I didn't plan to do much other than eat some decent food and rest in a good bed, but I was worried. The trial was very one-sided, and the jury was showing signs of disliking us.

There was no way I was letting anyone see my concern, however. Instead, I allowed myself to be escorted out, and the three of us were driven away from the courthouse, Zephyr having to fly once more.

It was raining, and he was less than impressed when it took almost an hour to get us up to the room and through the balcony doors. In the end, they had to remove a post that sat between the doors for Zephyr to get inside without damaging the frame. He still had to squeeze, but I immediately went to him and rested my head on his shoulder.

It felt good to have him close again. I wished I could promise never to be away from each other like we had been in the jail. However, there was a chance I couldn't keep that promise.

We ordered pizza, grateful to find that the hotel was willing to accommodate pretty much any request, and settled in for the night. There were cops outside our hotel room and more on the street below. Of course, if we'd wanted to leave, we could easily have done so, but that wasn't the point.

I'm worried, I said into Zephyr's and Sen's heads while we rested, our stomachs full.

Me too, Zephyr agreed. *This doesn't feel like a fair trial.*

What are we going to do if we find it's rigged in some way?

We need to be careful, but we'd have to find another way to prove our innocence. It's better if we don't have to, however.

What if they find us guilty and we're still there? I asked. *If we think they're going to find us guilty, would it be better to leave before they can?*

If we leave, the world will think we're guilty and running from the verdict, Zephyr replied.

I sighed and nodded. He was right, but something about the whole thing wasn't sitting right. It was as if our evidence was being ignored. Even Robert wasn't getting through to the jury. The case was going to be tried over three days. We had another one to get through before we had to decide to face our fate or force an alternative.

With this in mind, we all tried to get some sleep. I curled up beside Zephyr, all of us on the floor. His tail was both a pillow and a blanket and he wrapped it around all three of us.

Despite the impending threat and our nervousness about not knowing the resolution, we slept soundly until the cops woke us in the morning.

CHAPTER THREE

I saw familiar faces as we made our way back into the courtroom and prepared for day two of the trial. Once again, Zephyr only mostly fit inside the room, but we could be close while Zephyr answered some questions. Then other witnesses were called forward.

The second day was much like the first, but if anything, it was worse. The hostility we were shown was greater, and more than once, Robert had to object. He became more subdued as the morning went on, and by lunchtime, I was sure we had a problem. I had no idea what had changed overnight to make it obvious or why even Robert seemed to be giving up. He'd promised to fight for us.

I knew there was little we could do to get to talk to him, however. We were supposed to eat alone in a side room and not talk to anyone about the case. Somehow I had to talk to Robert, though.

When the judge called a stop for lunch, I got to my feet.

"Your Honor," I started, thinking fast. "Today's line of questioning has reminded me of an incident that hasn't yet been brought up. I would like to discuss the best way to present this to the court with Mr. Johnson over lunch."

"That's highly irregular and not something I would normally grant. If there was something you wanted to submit in your defense, it should have been prepared in advance."

"It's not exactly in my defense," I replied, not missing a beat. "It's... I wouldn't know what to say and how much to say without speaking to Mr. Johnson. Others are involved."

"Very well. I will allow you to consult your lawyer on this matter over lunch, but if what you come back with isn't sufficiently important to have warranted this, I will find you in contempt of court and will have to impress upon the jury the likelihood of something being amiss in these proceedings and recommend it is disregarded, is that clear?"

"Yes."

"And you still wish to do so?" the judge asked.

"My conscience and true desire to see justice will allow no alternative."

The judge nodded, and we adjourned for lunch. Our lawyer gave me a strange look as he followed us to where we should have been eating alone. None of us spoke as we were brought a mountain of sandwiches and snacks, most of them for Zephyr.

"What was that all about?" Robert asked. "I'm pretty sure there isn't any new information you want to add."

"No, there isn't. We'll have to spend at least some of this hour coming up with something," I replied. "I want to know what's happening out there and why everyone is far more hostile today."

Robert sighed and ran a hand through his hair. "I shouldn't be talking to you about this."

"I shouldn't even be on trial! I think we all know this isn't a fair trial, anyway. I was willing to play by the book, but if they've already done something they shouldn't have, and if this isn't going to be a fair trial, then I'm not interested in continuing with the charade. Tell me what has happened since I agreed to be arrested and what I've missed."

This seemed to convince Robert. He nodded and took a deep breath.

"Well, Jacobs has been in the news every day since you were arrested, trying to stir everyone up against you. Telling people you can't possibly win, that the branch of the agency you are claiming has attacked you doesn't exist anymore and you're attacking other agencies. He's claiming you are delusional."

I sighed, not sure I wanted to know all that. It wasn't anything I could change, but equally, it was something I was going to have to combat if I was ever going to be free to be myself and protect mythicals.

There had to be something more.

"There's no direct proof that the trial has been rigged, but... I just had two more witnesses I wanted to call denied at the last moment, and a third one pulled out. She was paid a visit by Jacobs last night. She had enough courage to tell me that, but not enough to stick up for you. Also, Minsheng called me. There's more agent activity around the Sanctuary again. They're still trying to find it. Ronan was going to take the stand. He now can't leave the Sanctuary."

I nodded, sure this was deliberate. "And the jury? Zephyr and I are getting looks that make it clear that we're hated."

"I've got no proof, again, but I'm pretty sure they were visited. Your organization folks, the ones who are paying me, have resources. I got a call from someone last night who said they'd seen agents going into the hotel where the jury are staying. A lot of agents. He got a photo of that, but it's not enough to prove they were visiting the jury."

I got up, suddenly unable to eat. This was far worse than I'd feared. There was no way we were going to get a fair trial.

Shitsticks, Zephyr said, making me chuckle.

Robert looked at me, but I didn't explain.

"Right, well, we've got this afternoon to try to turn this around, and it's going to be difficult. First things first, we need to figure out what we're going to tell them I was worried about."

Robert sat back, picked up a sandwich, and began munching. "Did you have anything in mind at all? It ought to be something that happened that night."

I frowned and sat down as well, but I still couldn't eat yet.

Eat, Zephyr said. *We might need your powers before today is out.*

It was a good point. I picked up the most appetizing-looking option and forced myself to take a bite while I thought. For the rest of the hour, we discussed all sorts of possibilities, from what happened that night and what I could have suddenly remembered I'd done. None of them were ideal, but I had to pick one.

I felt incredibly nervous as we went back into the courtroom. This felt like the make-or-break moment, and I knew if this didn't work we were going to be in serious trouble.

The emotions pouring through me ranged from fear to anger to sadness at how broken the justice system was, making me shake as I took the stand again.

Robert got up, thankfully able to lead this first bit. "Okay, Aella, in your own words, please tell the court what you remembered earlier and why it was plaguing you."

"Thank you," I said. "I can't say how bad it would be considered, but it is something I now regret doing. During the rescue mission on the compound on the night in question, I mentioned that we liberated the elves and took them back to the Sanctuary. It wasn't all we did."

I looked at the jury members as I paused, noticing quite a few of them had their arms crossed. Others were wide-eyed, perhaps a little scared. I sighed and continued, not sure anything was worth trying.

"I noticed they were storing data in the room beside the one they had the elves locked in. I had a friend of mine hack their systems, delete the data, and wipe everything. It seemed like the right thing to do at the time since they'd gained all that information by enslaving mythicals. But there was information that could have helped people, maybe led to technology. It might even have saved lives. I regret what I cost humanity by destroying that."

I nodded at Robert to let him know I was done, and he looked at the judge and the lawyer for the opposing counsel before sitting down.

"Is that it?" the judge asked.

Again I nodded, but it wasn't a good place to begin. My gamble hadn't paid off.

You tried, Zephyr reminded me. *That's all we can do.*

The opposing counsel got to her feet, looking smug. "So, Aella, you mean to tell us that your sole reason for talking to your lawyer was because you wanted to tell us that and didn't want to incriminate someone else? It was not much of a confession. We've no way to know that data was worth anything except your word for it, so why don't you tell us what you and your lawyer were talking about?"

"Objection," Robert said. "Doesn't relate to the crime she's being charged with."

"I think it does," the judge replied. "I'm not happy with the explanation either. Answer the question, please."

I looked at the two women and then at the jury. Even the guy on the end who had appeared calm yesterday was sitting forward.

You both okay with me doing something crazy? I asked Zephyr and Sen.

I trust you, he replied and shifted.

Sen trust, the small dryad added.

"Then I will tell the truth. I noticed a difference this morning. The cops looked at me like I was dirt, and every member of the jury's body language has changed. It also turns out that agents visited every single one of them last night. I wanted to talk to my lawyer because I don't believe this is justice anymore."

"Do you have proof of any one of those accusations?" the opposing counsel asked me.

I shook my head. "No. If I had proof, trust me, you'd know about it, and I'd no longer be standing here."

"So let me get this straight. You've just admitted to perjury as well as—"

"No," I interrupted. "All I've done is tell you that I believe the jury has been influenced, but I have no proof. I believe my arrest and this entire trial is a setup. I'm starting to regret that I allowed it."

"You've said that before, that you 'allowed' yourself to be arrested. But you didn't have a choice, did you? You might think you're very powerful, but you can't avoid the law. Not forever. No one can. You're a murderer, and you're trying to evade the consequences any way you can."

"I am not a killer," I said as I reached for the air in the room and manipulated it, separating the hot and cold. "I could kill every single one of you in this room within seconds if I wanted to, yet here I stand, asking you to make sure this trial is fair and telling you I believe it's not."

"Yet you have no proof of either statement," the lawyer said, standing near the jury.

I didn't respond in words. Sen hurried over and landed on my shoulder before grabbing my hair. I set the air spinning, twisting it tighter and tighter. Paper fluttered as it grew in strength, dust was sucked into it, and Zephyr exhaled a small amount of paralyzing vapor.

Reaching for the vapor with my mind, I pulled it into the tornado.

No one spoke as the twister grew. The paper flew into it, and the judge's gavel followed a moment later. Their eyes widened, and some of the jury moved back.

The cops pulled their guns, but I blasted every single one out of their hands. Then I started to show off, bringing the wood in the benches back to life. Plants began to grow at an alarming rate, and even Robert had to get up and move as the courtroom was transformed.

As soon as he was out of the way, I moved the twister until it ripped up the table he'd been sitting at. One of the pieces went flying out of the twister at an angle toward the judge. I stopped it, reaching for the air and slowing the hunk of wood before I dropped it back to the floor.

Keeping it all going, I looked at the lawyer for the opposing side.

"I could kill every single one of you. I'm more powerful than you believe, and I grow more powerful every day. But I don't want to kill anyone, and I'm getting really tired of saying it."

I made the tornado die down, keeping it controlled. At the same time, I tapered the plants I'd grown into neat and pretty decorations, not knowing how to get rid of them.

Make sure they also know this isn't a threat, Zephyr's voice came into my head. I looked around at the faces and noticed quite a few of them were wide-eyed and fearful.

"Please don't take that as a threat," I said. "I wouldn't kill any of you no matter what happens today, just as I tried not to kill anyone or let anyone die the night we rescued those elves. But I want a fair trial, and I'm not convinced I'm going to get one here."

There was silence as I finished speaking, and I wondered what they were all going to do next. The cops slowly retrieved their weapons, and I didn't stop them. It surprised me when they holstered them. Robert found the judge's gavel, but before he could do anything with it, I used my powers to lift it out of his hands and return it to the judge.

A moment later, I'd picked up most of the rest of the debris the twister had left and gathered it into a neat pile. The table was broken, so I put all the papers on another table and pushed Zephyr's vapor up to the ceiling, where it would break down and become inert.

"It is clear, Miss Carter, that you indeed possess powers that cannot be explained, but this is my courtroom, and I insist you never do that again while you're in it," the judge said.

I tried not to laugh at the way she'd made the statement, working to appear calm. "As you wish, Your Honor. I respect that you're just doing your job, as were the police when they arrested me."

"I'd like the record to reflect that Aella's use of power clearly demonstrated that she was here of her own free will and could have resisted arrest with ease," Robert stood and said.

The judge looked thoughtful for a moment, then nodded.

I watched the chill jury guy grin and kick back again. He thought the show was over.

"You may step down from the stand," the judge said. "We'll move on with the proceedings."

"What about the jury being visited by agents? What about all the witnesses we've had denied and the others who were harassed?" I demanded, not moving from the witness stand.

"You have no proof. I denied witnesses based on my judgment. Unless you're also accusing me of being bought or threatened, you'll get down, and we'll continue with this case. Your powers and whatever it is your dragon is capable of are impressive, but we're not going to entertain the rest of your tricks."

I walked away from the stand, went back to Zephyr, and wondered what I had to do to get the people in the room to take me seriously.

It was worth a try, Zephyr said. *Let's see how the rest of the day plays out.*

There was nothing else we could do without becoming fugitives then and there, but the afternoon wore on, and every witness made one thing clear. Jacobs had laid a very thorough trap for us the night we'd freed all those elves.

And we'd walked right into it.

CHAPTER FOUR

I exhaled as Zephyr joined Sen and me at the hotel. It was good to be somewhere we felt safe. I reminded myself I still had the device Chris had shoved into my bracers. I wondered if they could hear me. I was going to need some help if we were going to do what I thought we were.

We acted normal at first, ordering and eating dinner. I made sure I ate as much as I could stomach, then I ordered anything I could think of that came in a packet. I had no idea how much magic I was going to need. I'd pushed myself hard at the courthouse earlier, and I didn't want to be caught short.

I'd had the rest of the afternoon to rest after that, but I didn't believe for one second that we were going to be found innocent. Not anymore. Despite our display and our confession that we knew what was going on and the lack of denial on the part of anyone there, they'd continued to refuse us witnesses, and they'd even told Robert to shut up on more than one occasion.

It was a farce, nothing about the trial in order or as it

should be. Robert had given me a look as we'd left that spoke a thousand apologies. He'd done all he could or was going to do for me. If he said anything to anyone outside the courtroom, he could lose his license and job for breaching the rules surrounding the kind of trial I was under.

Even though I wanted to, I couldn't bring myself to ask that of him. It was unlikely to prove helpful enough to be worth asking him to do it, and I wasn't going to ruin yet another person's life when there was no guarantee it would be worth it.

That meant we were on our own.

I'd have given anything to be back at the warehouse and able to ask my friends what they'd do and how they'd handle it, but I wasn't. Zephyr, Sen, and I had to work it out on our own.

We can find a way through this, Zephyr said. *If we're truly the group the prophecy is about and you're truly the elf who's meant to wield every element and unite the world, we can find a way through.*

I gulped. *Is it the kind of prophecy that could get people killed because it shows only one possible future, or is it the kind of prophecy that's guaranteed to come about because no matter what I do, fate will bring me back to the right path?* What kind of world did I live in, and what did I believe would happen?

That's a good question, Zephyr said. *But whichever it is, the course is the same. To decide on the next move and try to get it right. Then the next, and the next. If this is a world where our choices matter, we'll be doing our best. If it's not, we'll make it easier on fate and everyone around us by doing our best.*

Zephyr's words helped calm me. I leaned into him, closing my eyes and listening to his rapid, powerful dragon heartbeat. *I would give anything to be back in those early secret days when you were the size of a large dog and we'd spend whole afternoons lazing around at the restaurants, reading books, learning stuff, and feeling safe and like we had a home.*

We have a home, and we'll get back there. As soon as we clear our names.

Assuming we can.

We can.

I looked up as Zephyr brought his head around and nuzzled me. Sen followed, bounding up and hugging my neck while she rested a twig-like arm and hand on Zephyr's cheek.

All right. We need a plan for the next few days, and we need to let the others know what's going on without risking being heard by someone else.

Talk aloud in code, Zephyr suggested. *Something only Minsheng and the others would understand.*

A code?

Yeah, just not Morse code. I'm pretty sure everyone knows that these days.

Right. They do, and they know other stuff, too. This would need to be something no one else but Minsheng could figure out.

"Why don't we ask the kitchen for chopsticks tonight?" I asked aloud a moment later.

"Chopsticks? Yeah, we can use chopsticks. But not too soon," Zephyr replied, both of us thinking about the first time Minsheng had asked us to use magic.

"Sen stick," the myconid added, making me laugh. This was crazy. It made no sense.

"Okay, so once we've got the chopsticks, we need...pizza and ice cream," I added, desperately hoping they'd understand that part.

"That's perfect," Zephyr agreed. "It will be like old times. When we were first together."

"Yeah. Remind me when we're out of this to find that wooden crate your egg was in. I want to see if it still fits in the case. You know, the bulletproof, fireproof, everything-proof one Ronan gave us when we first met him."

"Gotta keep that thing safe until we figure out where it came from."

"Exactly," I replied.

Sen looked between us, grinning as I visualized pictures of the things we were talking about.

"Is it hot in here?" I asked Zephyr a moment later. "I'm feeling far too hot."

"No, I think it's just you. Trouble with being hot-blooded, you're always having to do things to cool yourself down. I just get to go lie out in the cold or on the sand under the sun."

I fought to keep from laughing and nodded.

I think that's probably enough hinting, I said, half-laughing at what might happen and half-dreading it. *They're going to analyze this conversation a thousand different ways. If they don't realize what we need, we'll have to cope without it.*

We should rest until we can make our move.

I nodded, picked up Sen, and put her by my glass of water so she could take a big drink and then curled up beside Zephyr. I felt strange, knowing our plan had backfired. If anything, it had made things worse to let ourselves be arrested and go through a trial, but I'd wanted to show the world that we were willing to cooperate.

I'd never entirely trusted the government, but I hadn't realized how far the corruption had gone. Was it all the way to the top? Was there anyone left in it I could trust to help me? Or was I going to have to flee to another country?

There was no way to know for sure, but I knew I couldn't stay here and let the trial continue.

Go to sleep, Zephyr said about an hour later when I was still worrying.

His attempt to calm me only made me uncurl.

I can't. I keep thinking about their reaction to me using my powers. They seemed frightened, but...almost as if they were expecting it. Like...

Something isn't right with the whole thing. We've known that all day.

What if that was a trap, too?

It might have been, but what purpose does it serve them?

I don't know. I sighed and considered bugging the guards on the door to get us more food, feeling peckish again but not wanting to eat the snacks we were saving for later.

As I looked at the door, I noticed the usual shadows that showed there were men outside were gone. The hallway directly outside our room was empty.

Frowning, I got up, unable to feel anything but concerned. Were they planning something as we were?

I reached for the air in the hallway to see what movement I could pick up and then moved to the window to look outside. My eyes widened as I saw the empty roads around the building and the people moving out of it.

"We're in trouble," I said aloud. At the same time, I

threw up a wall of air around us, looking for possible sniper spots and trying to work out what was going on.

I think it's time to go, even if they're expecting it, Zephyr said. Sen left her drink and came to get in my jacket. I pulled the jacket on and stuffed most of the spare snacks into my pockets. The rest went in the small toiletry bag I'd brought with me, the only one I had besides the suitcase.

I was just pushing the balcony window open, Zephyr behind me, when something exploded behind us, hurling us forward and shattering the glass.

Zephyr's claws closed around my waist as he grunted in pain, and my back flared in agony. A moment later, we were somehow outside and several hundred feet above the street, Zephyr struggling to fly as pain tore through us both.

I gritted my teeth and concentrated on using the air to help him, trusting him to hold on to me. He banked to the left as gunshots rang out. I had to blast air away and down to protect us from the gunfire as Zephyr did his best to get us away and somewhere safer.

My hearing was strange. Most sounds were muted, but some were piercing.

It was a bomb! Zephyr's voice was loud and clear.

Are you hurt, or me, or both? I replied.

Just me. My scales took the brunt of the explosion. I protected you and Sen. One wing isn't working properly. I've got too many holes in it. We need to land.

We need to get far enough away first. Guilt filled me at my thoughts, knowing how much he was hurting but all I could do was focus on helping him to keep flying.

I felt him renew his efforts despite the pain, the heat in

it beginning to fade a little. Of all of the races, dragons healed fastest, but I couldn't stop worrying about him as I poured all the energy I had left into lifting us with the air.

Pulling up even higher, we hurried away from the city and into the suburbs, looking for somewhere safer as Zephyr took us on the route we'd planned earlier.

We were still a little way out from the back of Elysian Park when I spotted the massive armored vehicle we'd used time and time again, Minsheng and Daisy both standing by it.

I pointed it out to Zephyr with my mind and he flew lower, circling to check that there wasn't any danger before we landed. Pain flared deep inside me again, almost making me throw up. Zephyr was badly hurt.

Minsheng and Daisy rushed over.

"What happened?" Minsheng asked. "We heard an explosion, even from out here."

"They tried to blow us up," I said through gritted teeth. "Zephyr's hurt."

I tried to help Zephyr into the back of the armored vehicle, but he slumped on the grass, and it was pretty clear he couldn't manage that yet. It made me marvel at how he'd managed to fly us all this way.

"I need some light over here," Daisy said.

Immediately Erlan and Chris rushed out of the back of the bus, the young elf holding a phone.

He ran around to the back of Zephyr and exclaimed.

"Get him some painkillers," I said, knowing I needed some, too. I was in pain, and the only way to get it to stop for me was to stop it for Zephyr. At least I hoped we were that connected.

Daisy moved around Zephyr, inspecting his body while I moved around to his side and the wing he'd not yet tucked away. There were more than a few holes in it. I felt tears sting my eyes. They'd hurt him so badly and I was so angry and upset that I didn't dare see what the explosion had done to the rest of him.

Instead, I went to his head and neck and let him lean into me, stroking the scales on his neck and pushing soothing emotions into him to see if I could help him with the pain. Sen moved to my shoulder to lean into him and do the same.

Over the next few minutes, Daisy, Chris, and Minsheng cleaned up his back and got some painkillers and antiseptics on the wounds he bore.

"It's not as bad as it looks," Daisy told him a few minutes later. "Your scales took the brunt of the damage. Hopefully, they'll grow back in greater quantities."

"What about his wing?" I asked.

"It might never heal," Zephyr answered aloud, his deep voice even deeper and his eyes blazing. Anger rolled off him in waves as he turned to look at me.

"We'll do what we can," I replied. "We'll find a way to help it heal."

"I'm not your gal for that," Daisy said as she put down a large gauze bandage and taped it in place on Zephyr's flank just above the wing. "But that guy at the Sanctuary with the animals. Doesn't he have a lot of winged creatures there?"

"Orthelo," I replied as I nodded.

Zephyr nodded as well, and I saw how tired he was.

"We need to get you into the bus, buddy. Think you can manage it?"

He nodded, then Erlan came to my side and continued to record video as I used my powers to give Zephyr some lift and make him lighter as he moved to the armored vehicle and slowly climbed inside. He just fit, and there wasn't a lot of room, but the rest could sit in the front if need be.

Minsheng came to my side as everyone else got in. "Where do you want to go? Back to the warehouse to get supplies and try to hold the fort while we push for an investigation into who targeted you?"

I shrugged, feeling lost. I didn't know what to do with Zephyr so hurt. We couldn't fly while he was like that. How were we going to defend ourselves?

"We'll need a distraction for you to get Zephyr into the warehouse while he can't fly," I said. "I'll stay here and bring the agents to me."

"Are you sure? That could be dangerous," Minsheng said, worry lining his face.

"No more dangerous than being in a hotel at night, it would seem."

My Shishou exhaled and nodded. "Be as safe as you can, and then come to the warehouse. We'll all defend the building again if we need to."

"Hopefully, we won't need to. Someone just tried to kill us. Again. While the police were supposed to be protecting us. I'm pretty sure that's grounds to not be anywhere but the warehouse right now."

Minsheng gave me a brief hug, then hurried into the front of the truck.

I felt a strange tug as Zephyr was taken away from me and I flew into the air, lifting high so I could keep an eye on him and also work out what would draw some attention. A moment later, people spotted me and pulled out their phones to start recording.

That would do it.

I landed beside them and told them we'd been attacked while waiting for the last day of our trial. I told them Zephyr was badly injured and I wanted answers. I told them how scary it had been, waking up just in time to know we were being attacked but not in time to get away.

Only when I was done did I realize I was crying and shaking.

As agents and soldiers pulled up, I launched into the air and sped toward the warehouse. It would have to do.

CHAPTER FIVE

When I reached the warehouse, everyone was helping Zephyr out of the back of our bus and through the front door. He seemed to be in less pain already, which made a huge difference to how I felt as I came closer.

While I'd been farther away from him and our communication had felt faint, the projection of his pain onto me had also been less intense. Coming closer had quickly brought it back, and I'd almost fallen out of the sky once he'd begun moving again.

Sen clung to the inside of my jacket, having tucked herself inside. I felt sorriest for her. She hadn't asked for any of this when I'd bonded with her. I could have warned her or stayed back so it didn't happen.

None of us asked for this, Zephyr pointed out. He was still listening.

I hurried to his side, not saying a word to anyone. I noticed that Erlan was still filming. I helped Zephyr climb the stairs, using my abilities again. He didn't object or try to stop me.

A little later, Robert appeared at my side.

"What happened?" he asked.

"Someone planted a bomb and warned the cops outside our door to leave. It exploded," I said, surprised he had to ask.

"They're saying you planted the bomb, and it was supposed to blow up the whole building and everyone in it. Apparently, there are a lot of dead people."

"There can't be," I said. "We were the only people left in the building. They even blocked off the road below and had our guards evacuate. That's how we realized something was up. We didn't get far enough away in time."

I glared at him. It wasn't his fault that they were blaming us, but equally, I was completely and utterly fed up with being blamed for everything.

Minsheng pulled the lawyer aside and left Daisy and me to get Zephyr settled in our bedroom and make sure he had everything he needed. I stayed with him until the pain faded to a reasonable level and he closed his eyes. Sleep was the best thing for him right now. I could only hope the healing process was quick enough that he was back on his feet soon.

As I made my way downstairs, Sen was brave enough to poke her head out the top of my jacket again, but she didn't leave the safe burrow.

As soon as I reached the kitchen, Emily handed me a hot chocolate, and everyone gave me hugs. I cried again, relieved to see all of them. Even Crawley hugged me.

"Tell us everything you can remember," Minsheng said as he guided me to a chair and everyone sat down around the table.

I glanced at Erlan, who was still recording, and wanted to rant about how crazy it was that we needed to document everything. However, I knew it was the only defense we had against all the accusations and the lies being told about us. Record everything and make it public. So little of my life was now mine.

Despite being in my own warehouse and having been almost assassinated, as I told my story, a commotion grew outside. The reporters, TV news crews, and newspaper reporters had worked out where I was. They yelled questions from outside, asking if they could get an interview or find out for sure where I was.

After the knocking interrupted me for the fifth time, Minsheng got to his feet and went to the door.

"Look, folks. If I knew where Aella was, I wouldn't tell you, but I'm going to say this. Someone just tried to blow her and Zephyr up. They'll both live, but they're not going to be answering questions any time soon."

"Are they badly hurt?" I heard one of the reporters shoot back.

"Badly enough that they needed medical treatment, but not so bad they can't defend themselves if attacked again."

I grinned at the diplomatic answer and was immediately grateful for my friends and allies. Everything felt easier with people to help me think and plan. I tried not to worry about anything else for the moment other than getting through Zephyr healing.

The truth was that I was probably still supposed to be locked up somewhere, but I think we all knew I wasn't going back.

Minsheng didn't answer any more questions, despite

the reporters trying to get him to respond. He merely shut the door on them and came back into the kitchen. After I thanked him, he sat down, and we all looked at each other.

"You're not going back for that stupid trial," Daisy said.

"I'd like to point out that refusing would give them every reason to use force," Robert said. "It's my duty to do so and to distance myself from anything illegal."

"You'd best leave then. They've already used force, and I'm not going anywhere with anyone who answers to the US government right now," I replied. He frowned but got up.

"Do you really think it was a sanctioned attack from somewhere in the system?" he asked before he left.

"Yes," I replied. "When I used magic today in court, most of them didn't react the way they ought to. As if they had been trying to get me to do it all along. I should have seen it coming. Everyone knew I allowed myself to be arrested, but they kept denying I was powerful enough for anything. I let it get to me."

"That's a pretty strange reason for them to blow you up."

"No. It's the only way they had of dealing with me. Either that or this was supposed to happen, and I was supposed to be blamed for it. But it doesn't matter. My next move would be the same regardless of why they did this. I know they did it. That's enough."

"Well, if that's where things stand, good luck to you. I hope one day I get to speak to you again and all this is behind you. You're going to have trouble proving your innocence after this, but if anyone can, I think you'll manage it. I'll be rooting for you." Robert smiled briefly before hurrying away.

Chris showed him out, also refusing to answer all the questions the reporters tried to get out of us.

"We need to go to the Sanctuary in the morning, or as soon as Zephyr can move again," I said. "But for now, we're stuck here, and we need a plan."

Inwardly I wanted to do nothing more than leave the warehouse and blow everything and everyone up, but outwardly I maintained my calm. A part of me hoped we could convince people we wouldn't have blown ourselves up. Would people believe us? I had to hope.

For the next hour, we discussed various plans and possible next moves. None of them were great. We all expected the police to show up again and try to re-arrest me at any point. I knew it was likely they would use more force.

The most effective way for us to fight them before they got here was to go public and make it clear we were attacked, that we had been doing what people wanted before that, putting our faith in the justice system. I got ready to speak, and we found a quiet space in the dojo for me to be recorded and streamed live.

Erlan and Emily acted as my film crew. They helped me get ready and got the tech set up.

Once again, I explained everything that had happened that night, emphasizing that Zephyr wasn't with me because he was too badly injured to be able to stand beside me and tell them anything.

I teared up as I spoke of how he'd saved my life, but I tried to keep talking. Before I had finished, there was a bang on the doors and loud blasts from outside as if someone were attacking the building.

"We're under attack," Minsheng yelled from above, confirming it.

"Attack? Without warning?" I asked, but I was already propelling myself into the air as Newton ran over to Erlan and Emily killed the live feed. I flew straight up to the roof, taking control of the air around the whole building and solidifying it.

I was about to stride out onto the roof when Chris came running up the stairs and handed me an armored shirt.

"Made of Zephyr's scales," he explained. "It's not perfect. I had to add a few of the ones we just...gained to complete it."

I gaped for a moment as Daisy appeared, carrying a helmet that was also covered in large, bronze dragon scales. It looked almost molded.

"I've been collecting the scales Zephyr shed," she said, jamming it onto my head. At the same time, Chris helped me into the t-shirt-like top. The whole thing is surprisingly lightweight.

"All right, get everyone into the rooms in the middle of the building and find somewhere safe to hunker down. None of you are getting involved in this. We're going to make this end."

"Nonsense," Daisy replied as Erlan ran up behind her. "We're going to defend our home and our mythicals. You'd do the same for us."

I tried to think of a way to persuade her to stay safe

instead of fighting, but another loud bang made it clear I didn't have time.

Walking out onto the roof, I looked for the danger and people attacking us. The moment I was seen by the masses of soldiers and agents below, they opened fire.

I blasted air at the people shooting, knocking them off their feet and many others near them.

At the same time, I reached out with my mind for any plant life nearby. I was going to defend this building until the US army gave up. With any luck, I'd keep everyone safe until Zephyr woke up. I hoped he'd be strong enough to lend a hand.

Growing plants closer and closer, I decided to try to act as the Sanctuary had and grew trees around the building, weaving them around the brick structure as protection and. While I was doing this, I created a whirlwind around the building. The agents and soldiers were knocked off their feet if they tried to get too close.

Occasionally, a bullet got through and pinged off the armor I was wearing, making me eternally grateful for it. My lower half was behind the brick wall that bordered the roof, and I mentally thanked whoever had designed our expansion with that in mind.

It meant the only vulnerable part of me currently was a small portion of my face and neck. I thickened the air in those areas, determined that I'd stand here as long as I could.

Although the use of my magic was draining me, once I'd set it in motion, it needed only a little encouragement to keep going. For the moment, the air was working as a protective barrier, as were the plants growing around the building. I stepped back and looked for one of the others.

Erlan was there, his phone held out on a stick, Newton on his shoulder.

"Want me to set a fire burning around this even farther out?" he asked.

I couldn't help grinning but I shook my head. "Fire can get out of control. Let's save it for the last resort. We don't want to kill people if we can help it. They think we blew up stuff we didn't. For the moment, they're no different to us when we attacked that compound."

"True, but we did find enslaved elves in that building," Erlan shot back, making me wonder if the feed was live.

"Good point. We're still not killing anyone if we can keep them alive. We need tranks, and if Chris has any of those homemade gas grenades with Zephyr's gas in them, I want them."

Erlan grinned and left his camera recording while he ran off to get what I needed. I put my focus back on the barrier keeping the building safe and grabbed the first of what I expected would be many snacks while I stood watch.

Either realizing they couldn't achieve anything against my powers or because something else was on the way, the soldiers stopped shooting and stood down, heading for barriers that had been set up across the road for them to hunker down behind.

With the plants wrapped entirely around the building and the whirlwind no longer quite so necessary, I let the winds slow a little and simply kept watch.

I reached my control as far out as I could from the

building, wondering if Tuviel had ever had to do something like this to defend a position. Although we'd been training for situations like this for months, and the others would all be taking up defensive positions around the building, I was the main line of defense. It left us in an awkward place in the long term.

At some point, I would need to sleep, or my abilities would be taxed beyond my control. It was less than ideal.

Erlan soon came back with a couple of dart guns, a crate full of grenades, and other useful objects. Chris wasn't far behind him, although he stayed off-camera and merely told me what everything did.

"Can you make more grenades when Zephyr wakes?" I asked.

"I can get to work on it, but there won't be masses more."

"Do what you can," I replied before I noticed there was a noise coming from somewhere in the sky. They were bringing in the cavalry.

"Missile," Chris yelled a moment later.

Immediately I jetted air toward it, but Erlan was already moving his arms and it exploded in the air, a fireball lighting up the sky.

"Was that a drone strike?" I asked, shock almost making me lose control of the whirlwind I had circling.

"I think so," Erlan replied, shaking.

"They're trying to kill everyone in the building," Chris replied.

"No," I said, clenching my fists. "They're trying to kill me, Zephyr, and Sen, and they're willing to take all of you down with me."

"They'd kill me, Emily, and Newton the first chance they got as well," Erlan replied. "They might be pissed at you on a whole new level, but if every mythical in the world isn't worried about this, then they're blind to the danger. You haven't done anything."

"Is anyone trying to tell them that?" I asked, keeping control of as much of the air as I could out from the building to get as much warning of anything incoming. If anything moved within half a mile of me, I was going to feel it.

"Crawley's on it," Chris said. "Minsheng is talking to the organization. Neither appears to be having much luck."

I nodded at him and walked back to the edge, looking to see if there was a leader on the ground.

We needed to have a little chat.

CHAPTER SIX

There didn't appear to be a commanding officer, nor was there a single person giving orders, so I moved right to the edge and projected my voice.

"Less than four hours ago, I was sleeping in a hotel room and awaiting the final day of my trial. Then someone tried to blow us up. I will no longer submit to the police to be held until the trial is completed unless my safety can be completely guaranteed along with a fair judgment. Until then, I will defend myself as always. Go home before accidents happen."

There was a stir as if some of the people in front of me wanted to do just that. No one engaged with me, however. Erlan came close a moment later.

"Did anyone respond?" he asked quietly, clearly trying to get anything that did happen on camera.

I shook my head, but only enough that it would be picked up on the camera. "Doesn't look like there's anyone with the clout to talk to me down there."

I stepped back, not planning on making myself a target

if I didn't need to. It wasn't worth giving a sniper a chance to get me between the eyes, although I hoped I'd notice anyone close enough to shoot.

A moment later, we heard the same noise. It grew even louder as Erlan and I both looked for the missiles. This time there were two, but Erlan blew the first up even faster, and I hurled a small but powerful jet of air at the other, pushing it off course and toward the soldiers below.

They panicked before Erlan ignited that one as well and made it explode. The boom of the second missile made my ears ring and lit a fireball so close that a blast of warm air hit me and almost knocked me back despite my layers of controlled air protection. There were yelps of shock from the soldiers and agents below, as well as from the reporters who had dared to get close enough to film everything from the other side.

I made a mental note of where I could see journalists and their crews and tried to protect them. They would not necessarily know, but they were just trying to keep the world informed. They deserved this even less than the soldiers following orders.

"Might want to stop with the airstrikes," I yelled. "There's a lot of possible collateral damage with those things."

Looking out at the scene once more, I noticed the agents looked less happy about what was happening, and I felt rather than saw a pair on one edge of the perimeter they'd formed around the building slink off, possibly to do something nefarious, but in all likelihood to escape this crazy fight they'd been dragged into.

I pitied the rest, but I was going to hold firm.

Once again I snacked, but whoever was behind all this must have grown bored with the strikes failing. Or they were scared they really might end up blowing up their own forces.

Several helicopters appeared, along with a squad of fighter jets. All of them opened fire once I was in range, and I wished I had Zephyr with me. He'd make short work of them.

It was an intense amount of magic, but I used the plants I'd grown outside the building, forcing them to grow up even higher and swat at the fighter jets with branches as they came flying too close. I had Erlan target the helicopters' tails, and he set fires in the engines.

The men inside were quick to try to get out, and I helped them on their way, using my abilities to both save the people below from the crazy mess and put both the people and the carcasses of the helicopters down on the ground where no one would get hurt.

We dealt with three of the helicopters quickly. Only the fourth and final one gave us more trouble, the pilot wising up and trying to fly around while Erlan targeted the engines.

Still, it didn't last, and it freed me up to deal with the fighter jets that were still trying to get close to us. Erlan sat down, blinking with his head in his hands as if he was dizzy, so there was no chance of me getting any help on that front. I ushered him inside again to rest.

I tried to think of another way to deal with the jets and could only think of one.

Grabbing the few arrows I had sticking up out of the crate Chris had given me and the small bow Ronan had taught me to use, I flew up and matched my speed with a fighter jet until I could work out how to land on it.

As soon as I was sitting on the back of one, I used the bow to fire an arrow straight at something that looked important. It didn't make much of a dent in the paneling of the jet, but it was enough to give me some leverage. I took control of the panel and air around it, yanking it off and dodging when it flew back behind us.

With the jet getting too far from the building, I had to launch back off and then fly toward it again on the other jet, the two strafing back and forth from opposite ends.

I repeated the shot with my bow, promising to get some more arrows as I lost yet another. Once again, I popped the panel off the back of the jet, but this time we were still close enough to the warehouse, having started farther out and got to work quicker, and I was able to do more damage before being pulled too far away from the building I was supposed to be defending.

Stabbing anything that looked important and grabbing wires with the other hand, I attacked the workings of the jet until the pilot lost control.

As I propelled myself off the plane, the pilot hit the eject button and hurtled into the air. Catching the jet and the pilot. I slowed them both down and landed them to one side of the small army on the ground.

The final jet peeled off and didn't engage, the pilot not wanting to tempt the same fate. I moved back to the edge of the building. This time I heard cheers, and I noticed that a few people had snuck up to the back perimeter of the fight and were much happier to see me in the world of the living than the army was.

"I demand to know why I'm being attacked," I called again.

There was nothing but silence and the faces looking at each other. It was clear that they didn't know what to say or do.

"Was that explosion at the hotel caused by one of yours?" I asked when no one replied.

"No," someone shouted back, my abilities pinpointing him. "You planted the bomb."

"Why would I blow up my own dragon?" I asked. "Why would I endanger people who were being kind to me and then deny it? It makes no sense for me to cause that explosion."

There was more silence in response to my words. Was no one going to answer me at all?

I exhaled and stood back, waiting for the next salvo. I was pretty sure we weren't done and weren't going to be for a little longer yet. But what would their next move be?

For a while, no one moved, then Daisy brought me up a large bowl of chow mein. I grinned at her; she knew it was my favorite. I made sure I had control of the air so I could feel any movement outside my view while I sat down to eat.

"I can't believe you're doing all this," she said just inside the doorway. "You're truly growing more powerful."

"I had a lot of time to practice all sorts of different things that needed to be subtle and far enough away from the prison no one would notice," I replied. "It gave me the idea for some of this sort of stuff. Building things with plants, working out how to get something wind-based going and then feed it with the minimum energy needed."

Daisy grinned and gave Erlan a bowl, too. She then set a small bowl on the floor beside a shallow bowl of water for Sen.

"Thank you for all you keep doing for us," I said. "You put up with a lot more crap than the rest of us have to in other ways."

"I'll be on your side until the end." She gave me a quick hug before looking over the armor I was wearing. "We need to make this more complete, and I feel like Sen needs a tiny version."

"It's light. You could probably form a shield big enough for Sen from just a few scales," I replied.

"They're sharp, too, if they split," she replied right before her eyes lit up. "Be back in a little while."

I grinned, pretty sure Sen was about to get a major upgrade. The dryad hadn't done much so far in this battle, and I was pretty sure she was itching to help me. However, anything she did needed to be careful and considered, and if she got down to help fight the soldiers, we ran the risk of not being able to easily get her back on the roof with me.

As I finished eating, I felt movement, and I peeked over the edge to see the soldiers clearing one of the adjoining streets and waving something through.

I both felt and saw a tank roll through and park up, the gun trained on the building, and then another, and another.

I reached out with my mind, and the plants grabbed the third tank and wove through the wheels and tracks to keep it still while I tried to decide what to do with the other two.

Soldiers swarmed around, hacking at the plants as fast as I could grow them. I needed something extra. I was aware I was really starting to tax my abilities now, though. The beginning of an ache was forming behind my eyes.

While the men were distracted, I lifted a few gas grenades off the pile Chris had brought me, then carefully maneuvered them through the sky, unnoticed.

Once the grenades were above the tanks, I dropped them in and set them off. Although the men outside the tanks almost all sported gas masks, I was pretty sure the ones inside would think it unnecessary, not to mention a cramped enough space as it was, without making it even more claustrophobic.

I surmised right, and a moment later, vapor poured out as the men struggled to get out in time and not become paralyzed hunks of useless meat.

When it looked like they might escape this fate, I used my abilities to push the gas into their faces until they were all passed out as well.

Zephyr's breath weapon was the gift that never stopped giving.

As I sat back again, I reached for Zephyr with my mind. He was still fast asleep, and part of me was grateful. The ache from his back continued to diminish, and I had to resist the temptation to go check on him. Dragons healed fast, but not *that* fast. He was going to be injured for several days and not up to the usual life we led.

The final part of my thought made me sigh. It seemed it was becoming normal for us to fight so much of the time. It made my heart ache and I longed for something different, but there was nothing I could do right now. Maybe one day, the world would accept us.

There were plenty of thoughts I was going to need to

process, but while the warehouse was surrounded by soldiers, it wasn't going to happen. I needed to buy us some time. For Zephyr to heal and for me to think about who had tried to blow us up and what we could do about this whole situation.

The soldiers had retreated again and were either waiting for someone to do something else or taking a breather. Erlan was sitting in the small tent we had erected on the roof, and the look on his face made my mind up.

We couldn't stay here.

It wasn't possible to stay here, heal, and keep our friends alive. If we were going to work out what had happened and find Jacobs, Zephyr and I had to go somewhere else and lead away the soldiers attacking us, preferably unsuccessfully.

I was going to need to push them back and then make this place as much like a fortress as my magic could manage. Reaching into the earth below the warehouse, I began by shaping the foundations, driving them deeper and making them stronger, feeling for weaknesses and using the trees I'd planted to provide an extra protective layer beyond that.

Making the walls stronger came next. I filled the cracks, infusing them with metals I found underneath and generally reinforcing the building. I then reached up with the plants and demolished the tanks, pulling them apart and moving the armor plates and pieces to form a perimeter around the trees.

I swallowed most of the pavement for the fortification. It took a lot of my concentration, but I continued to eat snacks as I did it. The soldiers backed up even farther as I kept going, using everything in the area to make the building stronger and make it harder for the soldiers to do anything other than block off the street outside.

As I was finishing up, Minsheng appeared, bringing me another bowl of food.

"We can feel the whole building shaking with whatever you're doing."

"Sorry," I replied, distracted.

"Don't be. You're making us a fortress."

"Essentially. I wasn't sure I could do it until recently, but I wanted to make sure I could get out of the prison at any point, so I practiced moving molecules and materials around within solids, especially manmade solids. Don't worry, I remembered to put in some outer doors."

Minsheng chuckled and sat down beside me for a moment. "They're going to keep coming, and they're not going to let you rest while the agency still exists."

"You've been talking to the organization," I replied. "They told me."

"Good. They've suggested you go to the UK, where they have an abandoned boarding school you can use to lie low for a bit."

"No. Too far away. Have they got anywhere in Canada?" I asked, finishing moving the minerals and other substances in the dirt and earth around the warehouse and finally reaching for the bowl of food.

Minsheng raised his eyebrows but didn't say no. I sighed.

"Sorry," I said a moment later. "This isn't your fault. Promise me that you'll keep everyone safe while I'm gone, and keep doing what you were doing before you met me.

Save as many mythicals as you can and bring them here. I've made it as strong as I can."

Minsheng reached forward and pulled me into a big hug. "This isn't goodbye. I know we'll find a way to make it temporary. Keep everyone safe. I think Erlan, Newton, and Daisy are going to want to follow. Possibly Emily, too."

"Tell them to take my orb and head to the Sanctuary as soon as they can leave without attracting attention. I'll find them once I've pulled the agents elsewhere. Oh, and I'm going to need Chris' latest prototype."

Minsheng grinned and nodded before going back into the building.

"Can you keep an eye out up here for a moment, Erlan?" I asked, pulling off the armor and helmet and stuffing them onto him. I tugged at his hair and made him look a bit more like me. "I need to get Zephyr and my stuff."

He gave me a determined look and moved toward the edge of the building. I frowned and almost stopped him. He was getting close to danger to try to protect me, but I didn't want to leave the building undefended while I woke Zephyr.

I found the dragon already stirring, the pain flaring in both of us as he did. I washed sympathy and warmth over him, hoping it would help him feel less pain.

Can you fly? I asked as soon as he registered me.

As long as I don't need to carry anyone, he replied. *I'm already much better. Daisy works wonders.*

We're going to the Sanctuary for a while. Just long enough to heal up and see what the agency does next.

Sounds like a plan. It's not safe for the others if we stay here.

I nodded and filled Zephyr in on everything that had

happened while he was sleeping and packed my bag again. Just in case, I grabbed the few items I was most attached to and stuffed them in the bottom of my bag.

With that, we went downstairs and said quick goodbyes to everyone. I'd hardly seen some of them and I was tearful, but I held it together.

We were leaving to protect them.

CHAPTER SEVEN

Out on the roof again, I took the armor back off Erlan and put it on before adding my backpack and letting Sen climb into my jacket again.

Chris appeared a moment later with the new prototypes wrapped in a bundle of thin fabric in a pouch Zephyr could carry. At least, he would normally carry it. This time I slung it over my back.

Are you really okay to fly? I asked Zephyr.

It was still night, but there wasn't much left of it. I knew if we didn't leave now, while it was dark, we might not get a chance, but I also knew it was asking a lot of Zephyr. Not to mention that I'd not slept yet either.

I think so, but either way, we need to be in the Sanctuary before dawn, or we're going to have to defend a position all day.

I nodded. We agreed on that, at least.

Taking a deep breath, I reached to control everything again, getting an idea of where everyone was.

I felt some soldiers trying to find a way around the back of the building. I sprang some vines up near them and picked them up before carrying them back around the front and gently tossing them back behind their own wall.

Zephyr shifted his body and exhaled the largest gas cloud I'd seen him produce. He did it twice more and I moved the cloud over the people. I knew most of them were wearing gas masks and it would have little effect, but it would also help to cover our flight until we were much higher in the air.

While they were scattering in reaction, Zephyr flew into the air and I followed, flying below him and trying not to react to the pain I could feel through our bond. While I appreciated knowing how he was without asking him every five seconds, it made it harder to think.

The soldiers spotted us, but only a few shot at us, and I easily pushed the bullets away. We were already too high, which was what I'd hoped.

Zephyr flew toward the beach first, as we'd agreed. At this time of night, we hoped it would be clear and free of people.

We both flew there as quickly as we could, my abilities speeding us along with minimal effort from Zephyr. The ache from launching had faded, but it was hurting him to stay in the air. I felt awful for him and how much he was having to put up with, but there was little I could do.

Navigating together, we found a section of the beach that was empty and landed. I pulled the pouch off my back and took out Zephyr's heatproof covering. Without help from another person, it took me a lot longer to strap it onto him, but Sen did her best to help, and we hurt him as little as possible.

I could hear the sound of many cars in the distance by the time I was done.

Hide behind me and put yours on, Zephyr said into my head.

No. Get into the air. It's important they don't see you and where you go from here. I can catch up with you if need be.

I'm not going to the Sanctuary without you.

You don't have to. You just need to get high enough into the sky that they can't see you.

Zephyr hesitated, but even Sen pushed him away while I reached for the pants of my outfit. I pulled them on at the same time as I pushed air up under Zephyr's wings to help him get up into the sky.

He took off and I pulled the jacket on, getting snagged briefly on the new helmet and armor. It bulked me out a little, which meant it was a much tighter fit. I picked Sen up and pushed into the air as well and powered out over the water as soldiers came toward the area, shining lights and trying to find us.

Most of them had bright flashlights and were shining them up into the air, but already Zephyr was flying south down the coast and away from them, so they had very little chance of pinpointing him. I didn't dare turn his way yet, aware I was still too low and close to the array of people looking for us.

I flew higher and higher, getting colder and wishing I was on the back of the dragon. It had been a while since I'd flown so far under my own powers, and it was draining me.

There was no choice but to continue, however. Zephyr needed to fly independently of me so he didn't make his injuries any worse and his wing wasn't put under any more strain.

Fear and worry made my stomach tighten, and I fixated on my worry for him. It had taken one little explosion while our guard had been down to injure him badly and almost kill all of us. If we hadn't noticed when we had...

We noticed, and we're getting away from them, Zephyr said, his voice quieter than normal with the large distance between us.

As long as we can keep going, I replied, opting to turn in his direction. I would have to hope I was far enough away from the soldiers that none of them picked up on Zephyr or me.

I could still see lights on the beach as they fanned out to search, and more cars were appearing farther down, each one laden with agents or soldiers. They had a lot more manpower than we did, that was for sure.

They couldn't spot us, although it was clear they were trying. For now, it boded well. If they were looking for us elsewhere, there was a good chance the warehouse and everyone who was in it would be safe. With any luck, Erlan and whoever wanted to go with him would meet us at the Sanctuary before the next day had fully dawned.

Lifting higher, I followed the tug in my stomach that guided me back to Zephyr and away from the soldiers trying to hunt us down.

I heard the sounds of helicopters and jets as they also tried to find us, but we could fly quietly, our bodies giving off no heat signatures, and they made noise. It was easy to avoid them and make our way around to the south and then back east and toward the Sanctuary.

I came close to Zephyr again, noticing he was still struggling with the injured wing. With so many holes through the membrane, it wasn't giving him as much lift, and it only added to his pain as he struggled along.

At the same time, I was exhausted, and I was wary of helping him more than I could handle. It wouldn't help either of us if I ran out of power.

Normally when we flew, we kept up an idle conversation or we appreciated the beauty we were flying over or discussed what we were going to do about something. However, this time the three of us flew in silence. There was simply too much at stake, and we were too tired and in too much pain to do anything more than concentrate on getting where we needed to go, one wing beat and one jet of air at a time.

It wasn't the first time we'd been this exhausted after a fight, but it was the first time we'd been so alone. We weren't safe yet. Not by a long way.

The sky was beginning to lighten on the horizon when the ache in my head grew to the point I knew we weren't going to make it to the Sanctuary without resting. I didn't think we were too far away, however. Maybe another twenty miles or so.

Keep flying if you can, I said. *I'm going to land for a bit and eat. I'll keep jogging in your direction so the distance between us doesn't get too large.*

We've never been that far apart, he shot back. *It's dangerous to split up.*

I know, but I'm going to fall out of the sky if I don't land, and you have to be in the Sanctuary before the sun comes up. It's easier for me to hide in the daylight than it is for you.

We both knew my logic was right, but Zephyr still slowed, and I could feel him wanting to land.

I don't like leaving you, he said instead as he flew on and Sen and I touched down.

I know. I hate it too, but we don't have a choice today. We'll find a way through, okay?

Yes, he replied, the word coming out with enough conviction that I knew he'd be okay. We might have lost one battle and had to flee, but we were still going to throw everything we had at this war.

I found a small park to land in and let go of most of the air I'd been holding. The pain in my head eased as the unsettled feeling in my stomach increased. Trying not to worry but aware I couldn't afford to stop moving, I started jogging after Zephyr, using the tug on my stomach as a guide to keep me going in the right direction.

There weren't many snacks in my bag. I pulled one out and ate quickly. I was exhausted, but I had no choice but to keep going. We'd never stretched the bond between us over farther than a mile or so, and I knew we were going to need to push it farther than that.

The thought of not being able to feel Zephyr made me more scared than anything else. He was always there, always the comforting presence both beside me and in my mind. I might have grown up without him, but he'd been such a huge part of my life since I'd found his egg. I didn't want to go back to what was normal for everyone else.

Eating while jogging gave me a stitch. Trying to ignore the pain, I pushed on, running down the edges of several fields by a small road. It wasn't ideal. Anyone who drove along the road was going to notice me, but I wasn't going to deviate from the path I was on. Not now.

Keep flying, I told Zephyr as I felt him hesitate. The bond between us was faint, and the pain I was feeling from him was almost gone.

Can you find the Sanctuary without me guiding you? he asked. It was a good point. I'd left my orb behind at the warehouse so Erlan could use it, and I hadn't brought my phone with me. Not even a burner.

I'll find you. I know it from the air, I replied, trying to sound more confident than I felt. I didn't know if he'd buy it, but we had no choice. He had to get there before it got much brighter. Already the horizon was no longer pitch-black, and that increased the chance someone could look up and spot him flying in the sky.

If we were going to be safe at the Sanctuary, we had to get there without anyone seeing us.

With all my snacks gone, I continued to run, focusing on one task for a while. I didn't know how soon I'd be able to fly again, but I could still just about feel Zephyr, and while that was the case, I was determined to preserve my abilities. The last thing we needed was for me to run out of steam again when I most needed it.

Sen continued to hang on inside my jacket, her mind mostly quiet. I knew she was picking up on my unease, and she couldn't run as fast as I could, even if she could jump.

As the minutes ticked by, my link with Zephyr grew fainter and fainter until I couldn't feel anything other than an ache in my stomach where the tug of our bond usually was. I continued to run, pushing my body to go faster, but there was only one way I could reduce the distance.

Did I fly, however, or try something else?

Before I could decide, a car came up the road. I had been so lost in my thoughts that I hadn't noticed the sound until it was too late. I'd undoubtedly been seen, the beam from the headlights having traveled over me as the car rushed past.

The driver slowed and pulled to a stop.

Shitsticks.

I ran on, reaching for the air around me and pulling it in tighter in case I needed to fly or defend myself. However, when the driver's side door opened, a familiar face emerged.

"Aella?" Iris called.

I ran to the car, having never been more grateful to see the prim and proper contact from the organization. Whatever her reason for being out in the middle of nowhere, I hoped she'd help me get closer to the Sanctuary.

"Get in," she said. "And tell me where you're trying to go."

"I can't say exactly," I replied, knowing the Sanctuary council weren't going to be happy I was going there, let alone while I was being hunted by the government. If they thought I'd led the organization there as well, I would probably be turned away on the border.

"It is probably better if I don't know," she said after a pause as she buckled up and waited for me to do the same. "If anyone asks me, I can truthfully tell them they're not getting anything out of me."

"Let's hope no one finds out this ever happened," I replied, almost laughing at the absurdity of the situation.

She drove off, not going very fast, but going faster than

I could run. I still felt a sense of wrongness. I was too far from Zephyr to feel our bond, and nothing was going to be right inside me until I could feel him again.

I directed Iris, hoping we were going in the right direction and would be able to feel the dragon soon.

When we'd traveled another ten miles or so, I recognized a turning Minsheng had taken on the couple of times we'd driven to and from the Sanctuary.

"Pull over here," I said. "You've got me most of the way, but the car won't go much farther, and I need to catch up to Zephyr now."

Iris looked as if she might say something or ask a question, but instead, she pulled over and reached into a large purse on the backseat. It had another bag.

"Supplies," she said, "Courtesy of the organization. A special kind of burner phone. Use it if you really need it but not until then. A number you can reach me on is already stored in there. Plus a few other bits and pieces the organization thought you'd need."

I took it, lifting my eyebrows as I realized she'd found me intentionally.

"How did I find you?" she asked next.

I looked up and nodded.

"The organization has their magic, as do you. It's my job to find and keep track of our wards. I know we've not always seen eye to eye on matters, but you're still our hope for a better future, and you're a very determined leader."

I blinked, surprised by the respect in her voice. All this time, I'd thought she pretty much hated me.

"Thank you," I said. "Although I'd have appreciated

support in other ways at other times, when it's mattered most, the organization has been there."

"Nothing is perfect, my dear, but go. Get back to your dragon. I understand having the bond stretched feels very unpleasant."

It was all the encouragement I needed to get out of the car and head up the dirt track. As soon as I was a little way up it, I tested my abilities. The rest and the food had helped me recharge. I powered into the air.

Hold on, buddy, I thought. *I'm on my way.*

CHAPTER EIGHT

By the time I could feel Zephyr, I was struggling again and was worried I'd gotten lost.

Aella, he said, his voice a relief.

On my way, I replied, feeling the deep tug in the pit of my stomach guide me. I'd turned too far to the north, so I edged back to the east. It wouldn't be much longer now.

Are you at the Sanctuary? I asked a moment later, pretty sure he must be, but I wanted to check just in case. He didn't seem to be in as much pain, but I was still so far away it could have been the distance dulling what I could feel.

I'm there, and Orthelo has come to help. He's got this wonderful paste that took the pain away almost entirely.

I sighed with relief at Zephyr's words. The earth master was clearly also a skilled healer, and I was immensely grateful to him.

What about the wing? I asked. *Can he help with that as well?*

Yes, although he says it will take longer.

It was good news, but I was worried about his wing

nonetheless. I didn't know how long we'd have in the Sanctuary this time. With the US army and the agency looking for me, I doubted the council would want me there for long. I was a walking target.

We are, Zephyr said into my head, making it clear he could easily hear my thoughts again.

I smiled. Of course, I wasn't alone.

We talked about Iris and everything that had just happened as I flew closer, feeling beyond tired and yawning.

Thankfully, my powers held up until I arrived and touched down just inside the border. I couldn't see Zephyr, the dragon having gone deeper into the area, but Ronan was there to greet me.

"Come," he said, his voice deep as he bowed to me. I copied the same respectful gesture. "Zephyr has told us of the situation, and the council has convened. He mentioned that you haven't slept all night and have had to use your powers a great deal."

"I have," I replied. "I'm sorry I have come here with a target on my back, but Zephyr could fly no farther, and I could do nothing else to protect him."

"He's the last of his kind. You did the right thing to come here," the centaur replied, putting my mind at ease although I was still concerned about the council.

"I would normally offer to come talk to the council immediately, but I'm sorry, I need to sleep. I haven't slept properly in days, and I have pushed myself to my limits." As I said this, I swayed, and Ronan had to reach out to catch me.

For a moment he stopped, holding and studying me.

"I've never seen you look so tired," he said. "Come, let me help you to a bed. Zephyr is already resting in the guest house with Orthelo tending to him. I will help you there."

"Thank you, friend," I said. "I don't know what I would do—" My throat closed up at finding such calm warmth and lack of judgment. I'd almost expected to find them eager to turn me away.

It didn't take us long to get to the guest house. I rushed to Zephyr's side and saw the paste that Orthelo was still adding to all the wounds on his back where the bandages Daisy had applied had been removed.

"Your friend did a good job with what she had," the earth master said by way of greeting. "I've found that there are plants we elves can grow that can aid the healing a little better. It's been a long time since I've tended to a dragon, but Zephyr assures me I still know what I'm doing."

I thanked him as I sank into a chair near the door, exhaustion taking my legs out from underneath me. Only a little while later, Sierrathen appeared.

"I thought the council was in session?" I said as she knelt in front of me, studying me.

"Given you're the reason we have something to talk about but Zephyr came into the Sanctuary injured and alone, I thought it best to come here as soon as I could get the others to agree we needed more information. I am relieved to see you are here also. I feared the worst."

"I'm still alive," I replied, surprised by her look of concern. "I'm mostly uninjured, although I feel Zephyr's pain, and I don't know when he'll be able to fly again."

"Rest. We'll talk more when you have the energy." She got to her feet again and glanced at Orthelo. It looked as if she was asking him to report. He finished checking Zephyr over and picked up the large pot he'd used to hold the salve, then gave me a quick smile before leaving with her.

"Come to the council chambers when you wake up, and we'll meet you with food and discuss what has happened," Ronan said. "Should I expect trouble on the borders in the meantime?"

"I don't think anyone followed us here, although they might think to look in this area for us soon. Erlan and Newton are trying to come here as well. They have my orb and might bring some of the others with them."

"I'll have someone look out for them. They will be welcomed and given a safe place to rest as well." Ronan left before I could thank him.

I went to Zephyr and sat down beside him, leaning against him and closing my eyes for a moment. The salve smelled strange but also wholesome, soothing to the mind as well as the pain.

I could feel the relief in Zephyr as he lay down and curled his tail around all three of us. It took all the effort I had left to pull off the heatproof jacket and pants I'd put on. Sen dragged over a blanket from a stack near the side of the room and covered me up with it.

Sleep, Zephyr said. *We're safe for now.*

The words and his calm presence were enough to rob me of any more objections to the idea, and as the sun came up, I slipped into the oblivion of deep sleep.

I yawned and stretched, feeling Zephyr still beside me. His mind was still projecting the same strangeness it did when he was asleep, but I could feel Sen looking at something just outside the guest building.

Her mental images projected into my head, and I saw the sun setting and turning the sky a deep red. It was amazing to watch it through her eyes while I lay curled up against Zephyr and wrapped up in the blanket and his tail.

There wasn't anywhere near as much pain coming from the dragon's back, but my curiosity on that front soon got the better of me, and I got to my feet. My movement made him stir. He opened his eyes to check what I was doing before closing them again.

Have we really slept the entire day away? he asked as I moved around the back of him. The salve had soaked into the wounds, and already I could see the buds of fresh scales forming underneath. The areas that had been adorned with the green-tinted cream were shinier than normal.

Looks like it. I'm not entirely surprised. I hope Minsheng isn't too worried.

He'll understand. Hopefully, Iris will have let him know she helped us.

I hadn't thought of the meeting with the organization leader since arriving at the Sanctuary. It was good to be reminded. It made me less concerned, but my stomach rumble immediately brought my mind to another worry. What the council would make of us coming to the Sanctuary for safety. I was also worried about Erlan. Had he arrived while we slept? If so, where was he?

Zephyr got to his feet as I thought about this last question.

Let's go find them and then breakfast. Or Dinner. Or whatever meal it is.

I grinned as Sen came bounding down the side of the building and onto my shoulder as I came out the door.

Sen see friends, she said, grinning at me. At the same time, she pointed to a nearby guest house. Grateful the dryad didn't need as much sleep as we did, I wandered over to the building and looked for them.

Erlan was sitting by the window, also looking out at the sunset, Newton on the windowsill beside him, basking on a small patch of sand in the sun. It made me smile and feel better to see something so normal among the chaos of the last few days. With him were Minsheng, Daisy, and Chris, as well as Justin, Grim, and Ascra.

My eyes went wide at the sight of so many of them in one place.

Daisy rushed to hug me. "You're okay! We were all worried about you."

"I didn't expect to see you all here," I replied, feeling Zephyr's shock. Daisy went to check him over and made approving noises about what the salve had done.

Minsheng hugged me next. "We all talked it over, and Lyra is going to hold the fort at the warehouse. The second they realized you weren't there anymore, the soldiers backed off, and we just had a cop ask us to tell him if you came back. We assured him you wouldn't be back until you'd cleared your name of the false charges, then we shut the door in his face."

I blinked at the anger in my Shishou's words. He'd been frustrated and defensive of me, Zephyr, and Sen before, but the anger was new.

"We're going to work out what we can do here to help you and get this sorted," Chris added, pointing to a pile of tech they'd brought with them. There were several laptops and other bits of kit I didn't recognize, but I also noticed some more prototypes from Chris, including what looked like a bow, but far more modern than any I'd seen before.

I nodded and hugged everyone else before telling them about the council meeting. Minsheng opted to come with me and represent the group of mythicals supporting me, and the four of us made our way to the cave entrance in the center of the Sanctuary.

Minsheng hadn't yet been inside this new council chamber. His mouth fell open as he stared at the way they'd made it sparkle and lit it up from inside. It was stunning, but it helped to remember that when someone else was seeing it for the first time. If nothing else, the council and the Sanctuary citizens knew how to make things beautiful.

"I can see where you got the ideas from to make the warehouse stronger and better. Lyra said it has already had a positive impact on people wanting to come to the dojo. It's on the news everywhere, along with footage of you making it in only a matter of hours."

I grinned, grateful that the dojo would survive while I wasn't there. Business had been up and down, thanks to me. More than once, I'd considered living somewhere else permanently so I could stop hampering Lyra's efforts to run her own business, but she'd wanted me to stick around. In truth, I hadn't had the money for an alternative anyway.

The council was waiting, having noticed we were coming. Ronan stood among them, and it took me a moment to realize he occupied Lorcan's seat. The great centaur had died defending me on a previous mission, and I felt a pang in my heart at the knowledge he was gone forever, even though I was pleased that Ronan's commitment had been recognized.

However, it made it clear he wouldn't be coming back to the warehouse.

I bowed as I stood before them, and Sierrathen waved her hand to my left. I turned and looked past Zephyr to see an elf scurrying out of the chamber.

"We'll have some food brought in and talk while we eat. You look a little better for the rest, my dears," Sierrathen said, sounding more motherly than stern. It took me by surprise.

She motioned for Zephyr, Sen, Minsheng, and me to sit around a large picnic blanket, and she and several of the other council members, including Ronan, came to join us.

It always made me marvel when Ronan sat down. The great centaur folded his legs with grace and placed himself down in a manner that was both very human and very horse-like.

The whole council joined us, showing solidarity, and while we ate, I told them everything that had happened since I'd last been there. They'd heard some of it but not everything, and even Minsheng hadn't had the chance to listen to the whole story. The events of the last few days had moved too fast for me to keep anyone but Zephyr and Sen up to date.

By the time I'd finished talking and the council was done asking for more details, we'd all eaten our fill, and everyone was sitting more comfortably. Zephyr was finally pain-free, the rest, food, and healing power of the salve and his dragon abilities enough to take away the last of it.

However, I didn't doubt he was still unable to fly large distances or bear any great weight.

"This is a difficult situation, for sure," Sierrathen said. "We had all hoped that you could persuade the humans that we mean no harm, but it seems they have taken this worse than ever. I assume that while the bomb wasn't set by you, it was intended to appear as if it was?"

"Either that or actually blow us up. Either way, problem solved," I replied. "They are claiming we set it, given that we're both still alive."

"And once again, they're claiming people died when no one could have," Minsheng added.

"Perhaps it is time the Sanctuary left America, then. It is clear this country does not wish for our kind to be here," Ascra said, his voice full of sorrow.

"It's something I think ought to be considered," I replied, not wishing to sugarcoat the problem. "But there is still one other possibility. I find Jacobs and stop him from operating against us. Ever since I revealed our existence to the human population, he has been trying to turn them against us. I still believe that our best bet is to stop him."

"And in the meantime?" Sierrathen asked. "Are we to fight off all the soldiers looking for you?"

"No." I shook my head and leaned toward Zephyr. "I wasn't planning on staying for long. It would be wrong of me to endanger you all, but Zephyr is hurt, and I don't want to hurry him back to full capacity too soon. I hoped you would allow us to stay at least another day."

"If you wished to stay indefinitely, I think we would

refuse, but your desire to stay only as long as necessary to fight on and keep yourselves safe is something I believe we should allow," Martyl said, surprising me.

The fairy had appeared set against me and my ideas from the beginning. Perhaps we were beginning to come to a mutual appreciation.

"I would request that my friends could stay, however," I replied with a respectful nod. "Zephyr, Sen, and I will need to move fast and keep moving. We'll need to keep traveling alone. With your permission, I'd like to retain the communication stone that Ronan has given me. I still have it safe. If my friends can stay here and work on finding Jacobs, I will lead the soldiers away from you all to help keep you all safe."

"It feels wrong to ask you to do such a thing alone," Sierrathen replied, her eyes glistening. Vestan reached out to her and took her hand.

"While it worries me that the stone falling into their hands would be problematic," Ronan replied after looking thoughtful. "It would lighten my heart to be able to reach across the distance between us and know if you are faring well and keeping safe. It would also make it easier for us to help you from afar in other ways, as I believe we must."

I bowed to the centaur. It was a relief to have Ronan trust me. Now I just had to live up to it.

With nothing more to say to the council but more to work out with my friends, I bowed to all of them and concluded the meeting.

It was time for Zephyr to get some more rest while we planned our next move.

CHAPTER NINE

As soon as Zephyr was settled in the guest house, Orthelo arrived and once again checked over his wounds. He also checked over Zephyr's wings and applied a strange substance to them.

"The scales appear to already be growing back nicely, but I'm concerned about your wings," the elven master said when he was done with his inspection. "Some of the tears are very large. It's a lot of membrane to grow back. With time, it's possible to have the wounds close up entirely, but if the edges become too worn and are used too excessively in the meantime…"

"I understand," Zephyr replied, using his voice for the first time in a while.

I frowned, noticing the worry in his tone before I thanked the elven master for his aid. He'd already done far more than I'd hoped, but I was equally worried about Zephyr's wings. We needed him to be able to fly, but I didn't want the membrane to be permanently damaged by our actions.

"I might have another alternative, but I'd need to have a conversation with another elf. One older than I who remembers when dragons roamed in greater numbers."

"If it might help, we've got little to lose," I replied, reaching out to Zephyr.

"Then I'll hurry and come back if I can aid you further."

I nodded and watched him go before Zephyr put his head down again.

Tired? I asked in my head.

Exhausted. I doubt you're much better.

I'm not, but I've not been in as much pain as you.

True, but I know you've been feeling mine as well. Make sure you rest.

Once we've worked out what we're doing and where we're going.

I turned away from Zephyr and walked over to Emily and Erlan, who were sitting with two laptops plugged in. It was the first time I'd seen anyone use technology in the Sanctuary. I was pretty sure Chris was behind it as he checked cables, one running out of the guest house's door.

"Okay," I said. "We need to find Jacobs. I need a bunch of equipment to take with us so I don't have to come back for anything."

Over the next few hours, Minsheng made a list of supplies from the information I gave him and Chris, and we put our heads together on how to find Jacobs and how to clear Zephyr, Sen, and me of the crimes we hadn't committed.

It felt like it took forever. Meals were brought to us, and empty plates were whisked away. We made good progress before I finally yawned for the tenth time in as many minutes.

"Get some more sleep," Minsheng said. "You're going to need to be as rested as you can be."

I frowned and considered arguing. I also needed to get everything ready. Every minute we stayed while the world was looking for us was another minute that the Sanctuary and everyone in it was closer to danger. However, I doubted I was going to be able to get far in my current state.

"We'll keep getting everything ready," my Shishou said.

His words took away the last of my resolve, and I made my way over to the area Zephyr had curled up in. The large dragon was fast asleep, his wings tucked up in their usual way for the first time since the explosion and his breathing light and calm. He was mending fast.

It was comforting as I settled down next to him, his tail swishing over me in his sleep as if he sensed my presence even in his dreams.

Grateful for the constant warmth and companionship he represented, I slipped into sleep as soon as I laid my head down.

When I woke, I was immediately aware of the deep rumble of Zephyr's voice as he talked quietly. The words didn't come through at first, just the sound, then I was aware of Zephyr saying thank you.

I opened my eyes to see Orthelo there again. Zephyr

looked my way and I stood, feeling cold but otherwise okay.

"I've got to get back to my other injured creatures," Orthelo said. "But I wish you all the best. I wish I could have done more to aid you this time."

"You've done plenty," Zephyr replied. The elven master hurried away, muttering to himself and clearly somewhere else.

Before I could ask Zephyr what the earth master had said to him, Minsheng noticed I was awake. Sen also came bounding up and landed on my shoulder. The sun must have recently set. Behind them, the sky was getting darker, and the few clouds scudding across it were tinted pink.

"There are agents and soldiers nearby. They've fanned out from that base we hit the last time we were here," Minsheng said.

"Which means it's time to go and let them see us again," I replied.

"The council hasn't asked directly, but I think they're hoping you will." He looked pained as he spoke as if the confession brought him as much guilt as it probably did them.

"Have I got everything on the list?" I asked.

"Everything except the exact whereabouts of Jacobs," Chris replied as he handed me my pack.

It was heavier than it had been, and I was going to need everything in it. I noticed there were also more packs to the side, one looking suspiciously like yet another heat-proof prototype to shield us from heat scanners.

Daisy brought the rest of the equipment over to me, concern on her face.

"There are quite a few people who don't believe you blew yourself up," she said. "It's a good sign that public opinion is swinging in your favor, but you're not clear of all the accusations yet."

I nodded. It was at least one bit of good news. I quickly put the next bag on, using the weight of one to balance the weight of the other, although the fabric to hide our heat signatures was lighter than my main backpack.

Daisy held out another. "Food, cash, maps of some key areas you might be able to hide in, and everything Iris gave you," Daisy added. "Sorry. The food didn't fit in your backpack, and Zephyr said he couldn't carry any of it yet."

"I'll make it lighter with my abilities," I replied, not mentioning that I wouldn't be able to if I ran them out. I was more than a little worried I was going to be flying until I collapsed again. They didn't need to know. It would only worry them, and there was nothing they could do.

Ready? Zephyr asked me as I finished hugging everyone and Erlan promised to use my link to Ronan to get me Jacobs' address as soon as he could. Until then, our only requirement was to lead the soldiers away and then hide somewhere again. All I had to do was avoid getting captured.

I looked at Zephyr and gave him a small nod. Even though I wasn't sure we were ready, we didn't have a choice.

Do you want to try to unbond from us and stay here? I asked Sen, feeling like a monster for dragging her into this.

Sen come. Sen help, the myconid replied, giving me a warm fuzzy feeling. It calmed me, but I still felt guilty as I followed Zephyr out of the guest house and toward the perimeter.

For the first time, many of the council came to see me off, and they said their goodbyes warmly.

"I look forward to our next meeting in better times," Sierrathen said, taking my hands in hers. "I know you'll return to us soon."

It almost brought tears to my eyes, but I managed to smile instead and then headed to Zephyr's side once more.

Let me know if anything starts hurting and we'll find somewhere to land, I told Zephyr as Sen slid into a safe position at the front of my jacket.

I'll be fine as long as they don't do any more damage to my wings.

I won't let them, I replied as I powered into the air and added a boost of air to help Zephyr get into the sky. He didn't normally need it, but I wasn't taking any chances while I was fresh and his wings needed as much help as they could get.

Flying close to him and a little underneath, I kept my eyes peeled for signs of soldiers. We only needed a few to spot us, and then we were going to fly north and away from the Sanctuary, tricking them into thinking we were heading back to LA.

It wasn't likely to fool them for long, but as the sky grew darker, we would be able to find somewhere to land, don our extra layer, and then fly up into a higher section of sky. With any luck, we'd be able to fly east without being seen and find ourselves somewhere else to hide for a few days.

We were in the air for several minutes before anyone

spotted us. Swooping down, we feigned an attack on several soldiers as they combed the foothills for us. Thankfully they were still more than a few miles out from the Sanctuary, but it was clear they'd been closing in on the location despite the magic that deterred people.

It was a stark reminder that it was getting harder to hide among the human population of the world. It might have been a good option a thousand years earlier, but now, when humanity occupied so much of the space on Earth, there was nowhere that stayed hidden for long. My actions hadn't been helping, either, and I felt more than a little guilty.

While we flew, trying to stay ahead of the soldiers, they pointed at us and either called for backup or reported our position. I was grateful they weren't shooting at us, and the respite gave me time to think about where we were going next.

We needed somewhere we could lie low for a few days without getting caught. However, we didn't want the soldiers to be looking for the Sanctuary, and that meant traveling somewhere else and letting ourselves be seen.

As soon as Zephyr spotted more agents and soldiers coming toward us from the east, I used my abilities to power us both higher. It was draining to help him fly and myself as well, but I knew I needed to.

Although I couldn't feel any pain from my bond with Zephyr, I could feel a strange discomfort, and I was all too aware of the uneven gait to his flying.

You okay, buddy? I asked a short while later, reaching for his mind with mine.

Below us, the soldiers were gathering. We sped off in a

new direction. We needed to land for a few minutes and put our heat signature masking clothing on again, but we needed to get far enough ahead first, and the sky needed to darken.

Flying doesn't hurt as much, Zephyr replied as he turned, heading north. He appeared to hone in on somewhere suitable because he dived downward and gave me little choice but to follow.

A moment later, we landed in a small clearing in the middle of the woods. Once more, we donned our jackets. It was crazy that we had to go to these lengths, but as the sound of helicopters and jets sounded above us, the reinforcements called in to find us, I was grateful.

Chris was one of the least recognizable members of the group, but he had done much for us since we'd met him. I made a mental note to thank him and then checked Sen was okay as well, getting her tucked back into my jacket where she would be safe.

Ready to fly again? Zephyr asked me a few seconds later.

If you are, I replied, although I wasn't sure. I'd been using my air abilities both to fly and help Zephyr, and I was beginning to feel the strain. I'd taxed myself the previous day, and although we'd gotten what rest we could, it hadn't been enough.

However, we needed to keep going. I was aware of how hard Zephyr had pushed himself and what he'd fought through to keep us alive. I had no doubt he'd give everything he had if it would save me. Now it was my turn to show the same devotion to him.

Gently, we got into the air again and rose as high as we could without getting too cold. It was hard enough to keep warm, especially with the way the material we were wearing sucked the heat out of us, but for now we needed to keep out of sight, and the dark sky and the clouds covering it offered us the best chance.

The council has warmed to us, Zephyr said a moment later.

I smiled. Sierrathen especially had come around, and it had been a pleasant surprise to see Ronan being honored with his new position on the council. Why it was vacant brought a pang of sorrow, but it was a grief I had dwelled on while I'd been in prison, and the pain had faded.

It felt good to be in the air again. I soared along beside Zephyr, the effort to maintain the flight strangely easier with the jacket on as the updraft of the wind billowed it out like a sail.

Of course, it would have been easier to be on Zephyr's back, but there was no way he was ready to bear my weight, even if he was close to full-grown now.

I don't think it will be long until I can carry you again, Zephyr said, listening in on my thoughts.

But what about your wing? I replied without missing a beat.

Orthelo gave me some advice. I think I can find a way to help that. Not tonight, however.

I frowned, feeling a mental wall appear between us. Was Zephyr hiding something from me? I had no idea, but I was pretty sure I could still feel our mental connection in every other way.

There are people looking for us, Zephyr said a moment later, his head tilted down so he could see the ground. I wondered how he could even tell. The town we were flying over was little more than lights and moving cars to my mind. His eyesight was one of the advantages of being a dragon, however.

People on our side or the government's? I asked.

Hard to tell. There are civilians and soldiers, but they're not very coordinated. Could be both.

I thought of the town we were passing over and why there were so many people who thought we were here. It was a mystery, and it had me worried that the government had a way to track us that was far better than I'd realized.

It was a scary thought, but for now, we could do nothing but fly on and hope for the best.

CHAPTER TEN

It's no good. I need to land, I told Zephyr after a few more hours. My stomach was rumbling, and I was exhausted. We'd been flying for so long in the cold that I was covered in a thin layer of water, my skin slick and my hair hanging damply around my face.

I felt pretty shaky and had to stop helping Zephyr with my abilities just to be able to land in a controlled fashion.

We touched down in the middle of a large almond farm, the crop field still and quiet at the time of night. It wasn't a crop tall enough to shield Zephyr entirely, even when he lay down, but it would shield him more than not while I sat down as well and snacked on the food Minsheng had packed for me.

Although I could feel Zephyr's hunger, he didn't accept anything I offered.

You need it more than I do right now. I can go several days without food and still fly. You literally can't do anything a normal human can't if you don't eat regularly.

Thanks for making me feel useful, I snapped before I

caught myself. It wasn't his fault I was cold, wet, hungry, and a fugitive in the middle of a field of nuts. *Sorry.*

It's okay. I understand. This is one of the worst situations we've been in. But we've got to keep going, and we've got to make each decision with our long-term survival in mind.

I nodded. Zephyr was right. We needed to take this one decision and one situation at a time. Right now, that meant I needed to eat enough to keep flying.

Everything about the last few days made me think back to all the times I hadn't pushed myself as hard as I could in our training. All the times we'd decided to chill out and play games or read or whatever instead of practicing.

We trained more than most would have done. You can't second guess all the decisions you've made, Zephyr said as he lowered his head and rested it against me. *Tuviel and Azargad ran out of steam sometimes, too. It happens. Especially when the enemy has far greater numbers.*

It makes me wonder if we can get through this, I replied, wishing I felt more positive but not sure how to do so.

They wondered that, too. I think everyone does at times, but you don't give up. One moment at a time, you give your best and know it's all you can do. And it's enough.

I nodded. A part of me wasn't convinced. It wanted to point out that not everyone succeeded, but I pushed the thought away. I couldn't afford to listen to doubt. There was a chance we wouldn't succeed. I didn't know how likely it was that we would, but there was the possibility, and for the sake of me, Zephyr, and every mythical, I knew I had to keep going.

Stuffing the last of the snacks into my mouth, I reached

for the air around me. Zephyr spread his wings again, and we got into the air once more.

The tiredness I felt almost made me land again, but I pushed past it. We had to keep going a little farther. We had to get past our previous best flight length if we wanted to be safe for a while.

Chris had found a whole database on what the government thought I was capable of in the compound where they'd been using other elves as lab rats. They had records of the flights they knew I'd made and logs of the magic they thought I was capable of. Some of it was funny.

They thought I could control projectiles directly with some sort of telekinesis. They also thought I might be bulletproof. They also believed I was immune to the tranquilizer sedative they'd tried to use.

Finally, they were confused about Sen and Zephyr, wondering if Sen was a child or something I'd created with my powers.

It showed they were trying to figure out what my weaknesses were, and that worried me in other ways. They were watching me and had been monitoring me when I hadn't realized they were there. They'd tracked my comings and goings more accurately than I'd believed was possible.

The only good thing they'd confirmed was that they didn't know of any other dragons and had no idea how to hurt Zephyr. At least, they hadn't until recently.

I glanced at the holes in his wings. It made my heart hurt. He just wanted to live.

We flew east and a little south. The Rockies came and went beneath us, and we flew on. We passed over another large town, or maybe it was a city. My knowledge of the area was no longer sufficient for me to know where I was.

We landed in the wilderness after another four hours and rested, but I was spent, and with no more food, I wasn't going to be able to regenerate my abilities as easily.

What now? I asked Zephyr. *I have no idea where we are.*

Rest for a few minutes. I'll see if I can spot an open store.

Before I could respond, he launched into the air again. I tried not to get mad. He was doing what he could to get us through this. It was necessary, but I didn't like it. I wanted him safe by my side, and I always would.

The familiar tugging soon started in my stomach and only served to make my feelings of hunger even worse. This was a miserable way to spend the night, but I tried to hold on to the hope that it would buy us some time to heal and grow stronger while our friends worked on finding Jacobs.

I'd been sitting against a tree for about ten minutes and Sen was drinking water from a bottle when Zephyr landed again.

There's a store a couple of miles away, he said. *I could probably carry you closer.*

No, I replied, getting to my feet. Sen finished her drink, then retracted her roots and bounded onto my shoulder. *Let's walk, assuming I'm heading in roughly the right direction?*

Close enough. It looks to be a good mix of out in the middle of nowhere and used often enough that you'll blend in, even at this time of night.

Let's hope so, I thought as I modified how I looked. I had a few different items of clothing with me. I took off the heatproof jacket that was bound to draw attention and stuffed it into my pack.

I pulled out a hat and tied my hair up so it was out of the way. I would have to go in alone, pay with cash for some food, and hope no one recognized me.

My need for food was the weakest element of our plan. At least until we'd reached our destination. I had seeds in my bag. I planned on growing food once we reached our final stop. It would be a waste to use them before I could get there, however. The power I needed to clear an area and grow them was energy I needed to fly right now.

We plodded along next to a dirt road, staying on the other side of the fence. It was dry and dusty, but to the left of us, we occasionally heard cattle.

They were too far away to see, and they weren't spooked by Zephyr's scent. He kept his tail off the ground so it didn't create a pattern. With any luck, the ground was too dry for us to leave footprints on it, but there was no way to be sure. The cattle boded well for us. They could obscure any signs we left if they traveled over the area.

A few times, I heard noises and looked around, but it was always wildlife until we got closer to the store. The dirt track joined a road and it was busier by far, the occasional car coming down it even at this time of night.

Zephyr and Sen stopped, deciding as one that they'd come close enough. They hunkered down behind a large bush where they were unlikely to be seen and waited while I strode out on my own.

It felt awful leaving them behind, and I had to fight the urge to run back to them. However, we had no choice. I needed food so I could fly again, and we still had farther to go before we reached the destination Zephyr had in mind.

You'll be fine. Just think of it like picking up munchies after a night shift, Zephyr said.

A night shift, I replied. *One where I've been flying across the country.*

One where you're tired and want to get the groceries you need and get home to bed. Decide what you want to get before you go in and head straight for it. Comfort food.

Pizza, then.

If they've got something hot I wouldn't say no, he shot back, and the confession made me feel a little better. Not that I could easily buy enough to make him feel full. He ate a phenomenal amount now, and I wasn't sure how we were going to keep him fed while we were hiding.

I've told you not to worry about that, he projected.

You have, but you're being secretive. I don't like it.

It's a hazy memory. I want to make sure I can rely on it before making it the main plan.

I sighed and continued walking. I was considering using my abilities to move faster when I was still walking alongside the cattle pasture ten minutes later.

Thankfully, lights finally showed up ahead of me, and I made out a parking lot in front of a twenty-four-hour store. It wasn't very busy given the size of it and how many people must visit it during the day, but in the five minutes or so it took to come closer, a couple of people came out with groceries, and another person went in.

I slipped into the parking lot by climbing over a fence while no one was around, then walked to the front of the store as if I'd parked in the far corner of the lot.

After tugging my hat down a little lower and pulling some cash out of my bag, I made my way inside and headed to the deli section. I wasn't going to get much meat for a while if I was going to be living off the things I could grow. Along the way, I grabbed some energy drinks and candy bars that appealed to me.

By the time I had everything I wanted, my arms were full, and I was beginning to wonder where I was going to put it all. I planned to eat some on the way back to the others, but it was still a lot of food.

I looked for the self-service checkout counters and was grateful for the woman wearing a skirt so short I could see more leg than I wanted to as she chatted to the guy who was supposed to be keeping an eye on them.

I scanned the items and sighed with relief when nothing I bought triggered a check or any other kind of error. The cash worried me a little, but I fed the notes into the machine, and it whirred for a moment.

Just as I was panicking that it wouldn't give me change or was going to swallow my money, it spat out some coins and a receipt. I took both and shoved them into my pants pocket before picking up everything else.

As I was walking to the exit, I noticed the familiar sight of agents walking in through the entrance. I ducked into the customer bathroom for a moment and then poked my head out to see if I'd been spotted.

Thankfully, it looked like they were here to pick up supplies of their own. I had a clear run to the exit, so I hurried along as fast as I dared. A couple of times I looked back, but I tried not to do it too often and make it obvious I was spooked. They'd only be able to see the back of me, and I knew that would be harder for them to recognize.

When I reached the door, I looked for signs of agent cars, and the familiar shape stood out in the very corner of the lot I'd come through. I turned the other way and walked to a car on the other side, pretty sure I'd seen several agents still by their cars. What were they doing in this area?

You okay? Zephyr asked a moment later. *Did you manage to get some food?*

Yeah, but there are agents here. I don't think they know I'm here, but they're here for some reason.

Have they seen you?

Not yet, but I can't easily come back the way I got here.

We can meet you somewhere else, just get as far away from them as you can.

I exhaled and did as Zephyr suggested, grateful that he was calm and I could always talk to him. It helped when I was close to panic. When I reached the edge of the parking lot, I crouched behind a car and bolted down an energy drink and one of the chocolate bars.

I needed to load up on the calories.

With those both gone, I tucked the rest of the supplies into my pack and got it back on my back. There wasn't a lot of room, but I could lift it and get it onto my back. I looked around to see if there was a way over the fence and back onto the cattle ranch that wrapped around three sides of the store. I couldn't see any obvious way through. The hedge on this side was thick, as well as having metal paneling. It wasn't going to be easy to get through and leave no trace.

If I'd been able to use magic, I could have simply moved the hedge or used it to break a metal panel off, speeding up nature. However, I didn't want to do something so obviously elven when I was trying to keep my location a secret. It would act as a directional marker to our final destination.

The agents came out of the building and headed back to their cars. Instead of trying to look for a way out, I turned and watched them. None of them were in a hurry. They passed out the snacks and drinks they'd bought and then got into their cars, not one of them noticing me.

Making sure I was was hidden from view, I watched the cars pull out of the parking lot and head down the street.

Sighing with relief, I made my way back to the gap where I'd gotten in and hurried back to Zephyr and Sen.

So far, we were still safe.

CHAPTER ELEVEN

I suggested we land again as the sky started to brighten ahead of us.

It's not much farther, Zephyr said, but it wasn't the first time he'd said that.

I wanted to ask what he was expecting and see if I could get some answers, but I knew he was doing his best already and was as worried as I was. This was dangerous for all of us. He didn't need me questioning him as well.

After getting snacks, we'd flown on, and I'd eaten the rest of the food here and there, some of it while in the air so we didn't have to land again.

The area we'd passed over had been deserted, so we'd flown lower where it was warmer and easier for me. However, we would need to find somewhere to hide soon if we didn't get to our destination. We couldn't risk being seen this close to the place we wanted to use as a base until we'd found Jacobs.

While we were flying, we'd noticed another compound. There had been enough agency cars parked outside to make me believe they were the ones from the store earlier, but they were either inside or had gone home and left their cars there because there wasn't a lot of movement. It wasn't a highly fortified military compound like the previous two we'd come across.

I put it out of my mind while we decided what to do now. Every minute that passed increased our risk of being seen by someone. It would only take one human who didn't like us to report us.

There it is! Zephyr's voice boomed.

I exhaled with relief as he flew downward and followed along with him, not sure what he'd seen in the dark but willing to get on the ground and hide before we were seen.

Sen was curled up asleep against my torso, the myconid able to tuck herself away while we flew. It wasn't as if she was very heavy, and I knew it meant she'd be refreshed enough to keep a lookout while Zephyr and I both got some sleep.

As soon as we were safe.

Zephyr led us to a rocky area. Rivers had carved this section of foothills, and trees grew in patches all over the place. When he landed in one of the more spread-out areas, I couldn't see what he'd been aiming for.

The trees have grown a lot since my memory of the place.

The dragon's projected thoughts made it clear he'd been relying on a memory from one of his ancestors, a skill I still struggled to wrap my head around.

He led the way toward one of the hills and down into a gully. At the back of the gully was an overhang of grasses and moss, but he pushed past them and disappeared.

I followed, feeling him ahead and hoping he'd found

something as awesome as it looked. Darkness was my only reward as I followed, Zephyr invisible in front of me. If it hadn't been for our bond, I wouldn't have known he was there.

Reaching forward, I touched his flank.

I'm going to have to guide you until the sun comes up, Zephyr said. At the same time, Sen hopped down, seemingly able to see or sense her way.

With Sen projecting her vision of the gully to me from the hidden cave, I shuffled a little closer and placed a second hand on Zephyr. He gently moved forward, and I followed. It felt strange to be unable to see, but Zephyr took it slowly, and we were soon nestled in a corner that was a little cold but otherwise dry.

I felt Zephyr's tail curl around me, and his body provided me a warmth I was grateful for. I'd brought a blanket and a small travel pillow, unsure what sleeping arrangements we'd end up with. I pulled them out and wrapped myself in the blanket.

Are you going to be warm enough? I asked Zephyr.

Yes. It takes me a long time to lose heat. If I need to, I'll get up and move around a bit. Maybe even stand in the sun for a few minutes. The gully is well-protected.

I gave him an affirmative, my eyes already closing. I'd been awake and fighting for a long time with very little rest. Sleep stole me away from the land of the conscious, and I knew nothing more.

When I woke up, the cave was a little brighter, and I was able to see the rough outline of the wall. I was lying near one edge, still wrapped in the blanket, and I didn't want to move. Cold seeped through the floor below me, however.

Zephyr was no longer curled up beside me. Reaching for him with my mind, I found he wasn't far from me and thought it strange I couldn't at least see the outline of his large body.

Getting up, I moved toward him. At the same time, I felt the tug between us lessen as he also came closer. But where Zephyr's dragon body should have been, a man stood.

I froze, pulling in the air around me to form a defensive shield and preparing to bring the cave down on top of us if I needed to. He was dressed in nice clothes, although they were a little old-fashioned. The shirt and trousers looked like something out of a Victorian dinner party.

When I moved a little closer to see him in the better light in the entrance, he smiled.

"Hi," he said, his voice coming out deep and mature, familiar.

"Zephyr?" I replied, the name tumbling out along with my shock.

I moved even closer, turning around so he'd look toward the light. His eyes were purple, the same gorgeous purple as the dragon I'd been sharing the cave with when I'd gone to sleep.

"Yes, Aella. It's me. I've taken human form, finally. Took me a while to work out how to do it, and it startled Sen, but..." He motioned at his human figure.

He was muscular but not insanely so, and his dark

brown hair was chin-length. He had a strong, chiseled jaw and stood a few inches taller than me.

Can you still hear me like this? I asked.

Yes, of course.

I grinned and moved closer, reaching out to touch his arm. It was strange to feel the normal warmth of a human but know it was Zephyr. A dragon in human form.

This is amazing. Does it feel very different?

It feels very strange. It does mean I should be able to fly without my wings.

It does? I looked at him in surprise.

I believe so. I remember Azargad being able to use Tuviel's air abilities while he was in human form. He became something in between the two of them. As far as I'm aware, this is something only bonded dragons can do. It's in none of the memories I have of my dragon ancestors who remained unbonded.

Again I blinked, not sure I could take it all in. It was strange. If he'd been Zephyr in dragon form, I would not have hesitated to reach out to him, hug him, or lean against him. But like this? He felt as if he were both a stranger and not a stranger.

This is going to take some getting used to, I thought, meeting his gaze and seeing his steady look fixed on me. At least that part of him seemed right.

Zephyr reached out and took my hand, running his fingers across mine and the back of my hand. *You have no idea how much I've wanted to know what it feels like to touch you the way you touch me.*

Heat rushed to my cheeks, but I moved a little closer and hugged him.

My arms reach around you. I grinned, trying to defuse the situation, but it didn't work.

Zephyr smirked, and then he lowered his head and placed a kiss on my lips. It froze me to the spot, my heart skipping a beat and every inch of my skin tingling as if electricity crackled across it.

He gently pulled back, his arms still around me. I looked down, not sure where to go with the moment but not wanting it to end, but equally aware we had to start working on surviving while Erlan and the others tried to find Jacobs for us.

You should probably turn back into a dragon now. I slipped out of his arms and went to my pack to get the seeds.

If you're going to plant crops, I'm probably more useful like this, he replied. *But even if that wasn't the case, I haven't figured out how to change back yet.*

You're stuck as a human? I whirled and dropped the seed packets I'd been holding.

For now. But I'm pretty sure I'll figure out how to be a dragon again soon. In the meantime, I should see what I can do to help you make a vegetable patch out here.

I stared at him for a moment, not sure how to feel and worried that we were now in even more danger. While he'd been bulletproof, I hadn't worried about his safety. After the explosion, I'd realized he wasn't invincible. Now, he seemed even more vulnerable than I was. Just because he could harness air, it didn't mean he was as practiced as I was.

He had a point about being useful, however. If he could help me with making our mini-farm, I would strain my abilities less.

I nodded and gathered everything else we needed. It was a good thing I had plenty of seeds if we were now both going to be eating this way.

Was this the secret plan you wouldn't tell me about when it came to what you'd eat? I asked as we walked out into the cool evening air. It had rained recently in the gully, and the ground was wet. There hadn't been enough rain to turn the ground into mud, which I was relieved about. Our footprints were going to be visible as it was.

It wasn't a secret plan, so much as I knew I needed to attempt to take human form after speaking with Orthelo. He mentioned how it might be a good way to give my wings time to recover and spoke about Azargad doing something similar in an old story. I only had to search through my memories to confirm he was correct.

Can you search your memories for a way to become a dragon again? I asked.

I think so. I don't have a strong one yet. It's possible Azargad was stuck as a human for a while, as well.

Gulping, I tempered my feelings. I'd always trusted Zephyr and his abilities and memories in the past. I should be doing that now.

It's not a perfect solution, but it makes me useful now, and it means we can take care of ourselves better while I'm like this.

I didn't argue with Zephyr's logic, instead looking for a good place to begin digging. We didn't want our little patch of vegetables too close to the cave or too far away, and we didn't want it to look obviously well-kept. It was going to be a hard balance to achieve.

A little before the sun set, we found a location in another gully. The water ran down one side, forming a stream. A variety of plants grew on one side of the stream. They would provide us with an irrigation system and hide the vegetables we planted.

After handing Zephyr some runner bean seeds, I looked for somewhere to plant the tomatoes. I also had carrot seeds and a few seed potatoes I could grow, as well as corn.

It wasn't a perfect combination, but it would keep us alive. I willed the ground to move, creating holes for us to plant what we had brought.

Within minutes, Zephyr was trying to use earth abilities to bury them all under the dirt again, but nothing happened. He cursed aloud, something I didn't usually hear him do, and sat down to concentrate.

For a moment I did nothing, hoping he'd be able to get his head around using my other abilities. If he could figure out how to control earth as well, then in theory, we could become one of the most formidable enemies the United States had ever taken on.

Still, nothing happened.

Frowning, I reached out for him with my mind and projected my process as I covered up the seeds. It wasn't an ideal solution to the problem, but it was the best I could think of on short notice.

Much to my surprise, it worked, and he covered the remaining plants for me. Not expecting him to be able to do anything more, I fed the seeds the magic they needed to grow. They were fine until I had sucked the earth dry. Because we were in a more desert-like sandy area, the ground didn't offer much in the way of good, wet soil.

Zephyr walked to the stream and filled a bottle. He came back and tipped it onto the first plant, then the next.

It was a labor-intensive task, but I fetched another bottle, and while we were both watering the plants, I could just about keep up and grow them with the extra help.

We had a patch of potatoes, carrots, and the beginnings of several other plants. None of the plants on top of the soil had reached the ripe stage yet, but we were running out of light, and I wasn't sure I wanted to harvest them in the dark. As it was, we were going to have to cook a few potatoes and eat them with the remaining snacks I had.

It wasn't going to be the greatest meal known to man, but when I dug up two large potatoes and offered them to Zephyr to wash in the stream, I gave him a satisfied smile.

As we tromped back to the gully and our temporary home, I realized I felt comfortable beside Zephyr again, as if working together and being in each other's heads for a while had shown me that he was still Zephyr, and we were still an amazing team.

CHAPTER TWELVE

Sitting near the cave entrance, I leaned into Zephyr, his arms around me. We'd been in our temporary home for three days and two nights, and I was starting to get worried.

Other than growing ourselves some food and practicing our magic, there hadn't been a lot we could do. Zephyr was still stuck in human form, and although we'd grown closer thanks to that, I was beginning to fear he'd never be able to change back to being a dragon.

It was a difficult situation.

I'd dared to use the burner phone I'd been given once. We'd flown away from the gully, giving Zephyr a chance to practice using air magic, then I'd called Erlan.

The others had wanted to speak to me, but I didn't want to give the agency or soldiers too much opportunity to find us, so I'd stuck to talking to Erlan about their progress and made sure he knew where we were.

What he'd told us was playing through my mind. He'd

mentioned the agency base near us and that it was one Jacobs had been stationed at for a short while.

It might have information we needed. Of course, it might not, but Erlan had asked if we'd consider sneaking in and trying to get a copy of everything on the server in there—assuming it was the kind of base Erlan thought it was and there *was* a server.

My feelings were mixed. On the one hand, I wanted to help, and I had no love for the agency. On the other, we were supposed to be hiding. If we attacked a compound, they were going to know we were nearby. It was a huge risk.

Also, although Zephyr was proving adept and a fast learner with my magic, he wasn't at my level yet. I was worried expecting him to go into a combat situation would be stretching him too much

Have you had any luck trying to turn back into a dragon? I asked, still in his arms and enjoying it a little too much.

Not yet. I have to admit, I've not tried as hard as I should have. I like being able to hold you. To stroke your skin.

Zephyr ran his fingers along the backs of my hands and up my arms. A ripple of desire slid through me. I also sensed his desire for me. We hadn't done anything sexual, but that was the way things were heading. Each day we grew more comfortable with each other, and he talked about memories of Azargad in human form.

I tried not to worry about how that might change things. We loved each other. It was natural for us to want to take that further, but it also complicated our lives.

There was no way I could risk getting pregnant, but until Zephyr had taken on human form, I hadn't worried it might happen. I wasn't ever planning to be in a relationship with anyone else. But now here he was, able to do everything with me as Tuviel and Azargad had wanted.

I wanted to protect him the way he had protected me while he was a dragon and the way I'd protected him when he was a baby dragon. To take our relationship further but also to keep me safe as well.

In reality, we were two powerful magic users, and we were both getting more powerful as time went by. It brought a lot of emotions and dynamics to consider along with it.

You're getting distracted, Zephyr said, his deep voice gentle. *We're supposed to be deciding if we're taking on this compound, not thinking about us.*

I want to think about us. I don't want to just ignore the changes and what it means for our relationship.

We won't, but I'm not going anywhere, and neither are you. We've got time. I'm yours, and I always will be.

And I'm yours, I replied, feeling my heart swell at the declaration.

Then let's work out if we want to hit this compound, and if so, how best to keep us both safe but get what we want.

I exhaled as I sat up straight. It put some distance between us, but I needed it right now. He was driving my thoughts in directions I had to keep them from going.

Okay. We have several different ways we can sneak in, I said, *but I'm worried about us being shot at. We've only got one Kevlar vest.*

That's not a problem. I'm pretty sure I'm still bulletproof.

I blinked as I stared up at him, and he grinned.

Even as a human? I asked.

Even while human.

Are you sure?

As sure as I can be. I'm still a dragon. I'm just using magic to...look more like you. But it doesn't go all the way.

It explained a few things, but equally, it sounded crazy. It probably finished making our minds up, however. We needed to take on this compound.

Can you do your breath weapon? I asked, but he shook his head.

No, I don't think it's possible with the lung setup I have right now. They are very much human.

Yet you are still bulletproof?

It's not a perfect system. I don't know why I can do one thing and not another. All I know is that I think I can do one of those things and not the other, and I'm not sure why I feel so confident.

This was all the answer I was going to get. I felt guilty for pushing so hard, but I wanted all the reassurance I could get.

All right, I said, standing. *We should gather what we need and get going before it gets much later. We'll want to be back here before the sun comes up again, and it's already been dark for a few hours.*

Zephyr didn't argue. He got to his feet as I went over to the pack I had. I foresaw another problem. The heatproof outfits we had were designed with him being a dragon in mind.

I have an idea, he said, reading my thoughts again, another thing that was stranger with him in human form than it was in dragon.

He picked up the edge of the material that was part of his suit and pulled a section off. I heard stitches rip and winced. Chris wasn't going to be happy that Zephyr had ruined it.

He took the part he'd torn off and wrapped it around himself. Then we walked out of the cave, taking Sen with us on the way.

I tried to remember where the compound had been, but my sense of direction had never been a strong point, and I had to wait for Zephyr to confidently stride in a direction and then rush after him.

We walked beside each other for a short distance before he stopped and stared at his hands.

Time to fly? he asked.

I nodded and activated my abilities, pushing into the air. Hovering near the ground, I waited for him to do the same.

He was somewhat unsteady, wobbling as he left the ground, but he fared far better than I had on my first attempt at flying this way. Slowly, we rose into the air and looked around the area together.

Staying close to his side, I made sure I was there to support him if he struggled too much, but the longer we were in the air, the more stable he became. As he usually did, Zephyr led the way. Even as a human-form dragon, his night sight was better than mine and made it easier for him to guide us in the right direction.

It was strange not flying with a dragon beside or under me, but having flown all the way out here separately, I was less bothered by the difference. However, there was no doubt about it; I would need time to get used to Zephyr not being a dragon all the time.

Now and then, I felt him panic a little as he struggled to

control the air around him or lost focus. He appeared to find it instinctive, but he hadn't practiced much. He had watched me fly countless times, but he didn't have the muscle memory to go with it and make it look effortless.

It showed me how far I'd come and how much my training was making a difference. Using my powers had become natural. Flying was no harder than breathing most of the time. It wasn't so easy for Zephyr.

We flew on anyway, the small compound we'd seen the night before coming up ahead of us. Still far enough out that we were unlikely to be seen as anything important, we landed quietly and walked closer.

The fence around this base was almost nonexistent. It was more of a perimeter marking than something designed to keep people out. It was strange by comparison to the other bases we'd been on and made me feel sure there wasn't going to be anything here of use.

However, Erlan wanted us to find the information there, and that's what I was determined to do. It was imperative we weren't seen. They couldn't know where we were. Not yet.

Let's circle around and come in from the other side, Zephyr said, his deep rumble making me jump when I had his human form beside me.

It was a good plan, so we backed up a little and trekked around to the other side before coming closer again. I spotted several cameras, and Zephyr spied a few more. We got to work, using our abilities to disable them. It didn't take long for the guards to respond, some of them coming around to where we were. They pulled guns and checked out the cameras.

We could have done with Zephyr's breath weapon, but it wasn't going to be possible. Instead, I pulled the tranquilizer gun out and shot them. It took a moment, but all four guards went down, although not until after the last one had opened fire in our direction. The bullets went wide, but I threw up an air barrier anyway and pushed the gun away.

An errant shot hit Zephyr before I could trank the final guard and knock him out. I rushed to Zephyr's side, but he didn't appear to be harmed.

My skin is as hard as my scales, he projected. *I could even see them for a moment where I was hit, almost as if the human form is only an illusion.*

I lifted my eyebrow, but more agents had been attracted by the gunshots. They immediately noticed the downed cameras and their sedated comrades. We needed an alternative way of getting these agents out of action.

Suggestions? I asked Zephyr.

He thought for a moment while we crouched in the darkness beyond the men. I could see a few with flashlights, but I batted them away with my air powers and then hurled them at the sides of the buildings so they broke.

It wasn't subtle, but I wasn't sure what else to do. They knew something was here, and there wasn't much we could do about it now.

Want to abort? Zephyr asked as the agents fired their weapons again. Trying to hit something they couldn't see wasn't going to get them an advantage. However, it wasn't good for us, even though I was wearing the armor of dragon scales Daisy and Chris had made me.

We're here now, and they know it, I replied. *I don't suppose you could become a dragon again, could you?*

Zephyr crouched near me and closed his eyes. I watched his skin flicker, dragon scales appearing and then disappearing again as he looked human once more. Or at least, mostly human. His eyes were still a deep purple.

I don't think I can. I'm not sure why, but...

I nodded, not wanting to push him or make him feel worried. It was what it was.

Okay, Looks like we'll have to use some plants. I looked around but there weren't many, mostly cacti or shrubs of bushes that didn't have many branches, and I didn't have the capacity to grow them too far without a vine-like growth pattern. They would need water and nutrients.

Runner beans? Zephyr suggested.

That might work.

It would use up some of our supply of seeds, but I could always grow the few I had planted by our cave to maturity and leave some in pods to become new seeds.

Reaching into my pack, I pulled out a handful of beans and floated them closer, taking them up into the air and then lowering them where I needed the plants.

It took a lot of concentration, but as soon as the seeds were in the soil, Zephyr took over controlling some of them, and we grew the large runners upward while also growing the roots down.

They weren't the strongest plants, but working together, we used them to sneak up on the agents. In the dark, they didn't notice when we ran the plants along the ground, grabbed each agent, and lifted them up off the ground.

I used the leaves to cover their eyes or positioned them so they wouldn't be able to see us. It wasn't a permanent solution, and I was pretty sure it wouldn't hold for very long, but it was a start.

With all the agents who'd come to check out the commotion dealt with in one way or another, we ran closer and flew over the fence into the compound. Reaching the agents on the ground that we'd sedated, I tried to see if they had any more tranquilizer weaponry, but they were only armed with guns.

I took the guns and bullets from all of them and buried them deep in the ground with my mind while Zephyr kept a lookout for trouble.

There were only a couple of buildings, and one looked like it was a garage. We ignored the garage for now, only pausing to disable some more cameras before they picked us up.

We headed to the door and I used my powers to pick the lock, putting pressure on the pins inside so they'd turn.

Ready? I asked Zephyr. I wasn't sure what we'd find inside.

Yup. Let's go get our info.

CHAPTER THIRTEEN

I pulled the door open and stepped inside. The interior lights came on automatically. Zephyr came in after me and shut the door and then crouched. It felt strange to have him at my side. Sen was sitting on top of the building, keeping an eye on the agents we'd tied up.

The last time we'd attacked a building, Zephyr had been forced to stay on the outside. Finally he'd pulled the wall apart to come inside, and he'd had to keep destroying walls to get through to me.

This time he walked beside me, and it felt more than a little strange that I wasn't alone. The lights announced our presence, but there were no more cameras as far as I could tell. There were only rooms on our left. The corridor we were in headed around to the right rather than straight through the heart of the building, but we followed it anyway.

Opening the first door revealed a large gym area where agents could work out. It was empty. Whoever normally used it was either gone for the night or somewhere else in the building. The next door opened on a small swimming pool, the water calm and still. I shut the door and moved on.

We passed a storage room next, spare weights, and even a couple of basketballs in there. While I was impressed with the equipment, it wasn't the sort of thing we were here for.

Onward we went, turning a corner and heading even farther around the outside. This side had a few more doors, but only after we'd gone past what I figured was the back of the swimming pool. It opened out into a large open-plan office. I went inside.

Again, the room was empty and the desks were clear. I went up to the nearest one and tried to break the lock. I couldn't see inside well enough to try my last trick. Zephyr came closer and simply smacked the desk. The whole piece of furniture cracked in two with an almighty bang.

I whirled around to face the door in case anyone had heard us, but no one appeared. Zephyr pulled out the drawers. There were a few papers in it. Half-filled in reports on investigations into mythicals, emails about what a fire salamander looked like and how it was different from normal newts and salamanders.

We moved on to the next and the next, finding similar documents. This was clearly an office of agents similar to the one we had in LA. The agents were tasked with capturing mythicals and taking them somewhere else. If that was so, it made sense why Jacobs had been stationed here in the past.

The fourth desk revealed a laptop, and I flicked it open. It was password-protected, which wasn't a surprise. We searched the desk for something with the password written on it, with no luck.

Frowning, we moved on, but not a single desk had anything we could hack into easily.

Let's just take one and see what else we can find, Zephyr suggested, rubbing his hand as if it was starting to hurt after cracking so many desks open. I nodded, picking the laptop on the only desk with a nameplate. There was a chance it would have better information on it if it belonged to someone in charge.

It went into my pack, weighing it down more than I'd have liked, and then we went back out into the hall.

The next room was the kitchen.

I raided the cupboards for food, grinning as Zephyr bit into a donut from a bag on a shelf. His eyes lit up.

These taste amazing in human form, he said before taking another big bite.

We should see what you think of pizza in this form, I replied and took a bite out of one before stuffing the rest into my pack. Along with the donuts, there were also chips, teabags, and candy bars.

When the pack was full, I continued to stuff candy bars into our pockets. Some of them would melt, but I was sure they'd solidify once we were back in the cold cave. They would supplement the fruit and veggies we could grow.

With that done, we returned to the search.

I noticed a set of stairs in the far corner, and Zephyr opted to guard them while I continued to the last section of the building. The corridor ended in a large metal door that appeared to be more robust than the others.

I was surprised we hadn't been met with more agents, but there hadn't been a massive number of desks, and the parking lot outside hadn't been full of cars, so it was possible that there just weren't that many people here at this time of night.

I tried the door, but it wouldn't budge, and I didn't know the code to unlock it.

Reaching for air with my mind, I sensed there was a small air pocket around the bolts inside the lock, and I increased the pressure by forcing more air into the gaps to push the bolts back.

The door made strange sounds, something buckled somewhere, and my head ached a little as I increased the pressure.

Eventually, it gave, and I pulled it open.

Inside were rows of weapons and ammo, Kevlar vests, cages, tasers, and tranquilizer guns. I grabbed several of the tranquilizer guns and lifted the whole case of ammo up with my mind.

Shifting them out of the room, I tried to decide what to do with everything else. There was no way I wanted to leave all this weaponry here to possibly be used against us, but I wasn't sure what else to do with it when my pack was full and there was far too much to float out of the building.

Come back to it if we get a chance, otherwise fix the door in place so it can't be easily opened, Zephyr suggested from his position at the other end of the corridor.

It was the best idea either of us had, so I walked away and pushed the door shut again with my mind. I couldn't easily get the bolts to move to lock it again, but it didn't matter right now.

After handing Zephyr a gun and some ammo and stashing the rest of the ammo under the stairs to pick up on our way down again, we started to climb, focusing on stealth over speed.

Again, we met no resistance, and that made me even more concerned. Surely there should be someone in charge here or some agents who had stayed back.

The corridor on this floor went around the edge of the building again, but only halfway. Then it headed across the middle, forming a loop around more offices. These only had desks for a few people, sometimes one or two, and there was a receptionist's desk, one of a very few with a phone.

I also spotted some storage for office supplies, and a restroom.

It didn't smell great, but I ducked in anyway and made sure all the stalls were empty while Zephyr continued to guard our rear. Once more, we found ourselves to be alone.

Finally, we walked down the last section of the corridor and came to a door at the front of the building. It was ajar, and a light was on inside.

We slowed as we got closer, and I lifted my weapon.

"You may as well come in, Aella-Faye. I know you're there," a man called from inside. It wasn't one I recognized, but I did as he asked, leaving Zephyr in the corridor.

Who is it? Zephyr asked as soon as I was inside.

I exhaled as I trained my gun on the lone man sitting

behind the desk. He had pushed his chair back, and his hands were in the air as if he was surrendering.

No idea, but he doesn't seem to be a threat.

I kept my eyes on him, but I could still take in a significant chunk of the room. It was a largish office, with one room off to each side.

A large table in a meeting room sat to the left, and a small server farm to the right. We'd found what we were looking for. Possibly.

"What brings the great elven warrior to my office?" the man asked.

"Information," I replied. "I'd ask you if reinforcements are on the way, but I think we both know the answer to that question is yes or you wouldn't be so calm."

"They are, but I'm calm because we both know you're not going to kill me. You're holding a dart gun for one, and you never deliberately kill anyone."

I lifted an eyebrow. That wasn't the reply I'd expected.

"While most agents believe you murdered some of our team, a few of us have a clearance level high enough that we know the truth. You're being framed so we can be officially recognized as an agency again, a necessity to fight your kind. It's propaganda in a war and nothing more."

"I want it to end."

"I can imagine. It must be extremely difficult for you to be the target of it." He got to his feet as he spoke, his arms still held out. "Let me get the keys."

He moved to a small picture on the wall and pushed it aside. A safe sat behind it, and I felt wary.

"I'll open it," I said, hoping Zephyr had heard everything and was looking out for trouble.

The man gave me the combination, and I was relieved to open the safe and find a set of keys as he'd said, as well as a small stack of money. I took both and tucked the cash into the only empty pocket I had left.

I heard the agent chuckle.

"Emptied the kitchen as well, I assume?" he commented.

"Figured, why not? You've made it hard for me to go to a store right now."

"Yeah, I'd apologize for that, but I doubt you'd believe me to be sincere."

"Correct," I replied, holding up the keys to get him to tell me which one I wanted.

He described one and I moved to the server door, looking back at him frequently. The agent sat back down, resting his elbows on the arms of the chair and wheeling to the side to make it easier for me.

I tried the key in the lock, and it worked the first time. I strode into the room and went to the desktop computer by the servers. I powered it on but didn't sit down. The system prompted me for a password.

"What will let me in?" I asked, "I want to find information on Jacobs."

I saw no point in hiding it. He might know we were coming for him.

"Ah, my boss. There's not much on there, but what makes you think I'll just tell you? I'm going to get in enough trouble as it is for letting you have the server keys, especially since we know you won't harm me."

"No. I won't kill you. I have no problem with causing

you or anyone else pain. Especially when you're all trying to kill me and those I care about."

The man's eyes widened; it was clear he hadn't considered that possibility. There were two plants in the room and I took control of them, reaching out for him with them.

He tried to shift as one wrapped around his arm and the chair, but he didn't move fast enough, and I used the other to wrap the other arm and pin it down.

"You should just tell me," I said as I walked back out and closer to him. "I've not got a lot of patience, and you've informed me reinforcements are on the way, so I don't want to waste time."

He looked thoughtful for a moment, but eventually, he sighed and nodded. A moment later, he told me the password.

I hurried back to the server room and punched it in. The desktop screen came up, the computer running on an older operating system that almost made me laugh.

It was fairly easy to navigate, and I typed Jacobs' name into a search engine. It was a little on the slow side. While it was lumbering through the search and results were popping up, I stuck in a data stick and started copying the files and folders on the hard drive.

While it wasn't all going to be useful, it was the fastest way to get what I needed.

I think company is arriving, Zephyr said when I still had a fair few to go. *Cars are pulling into the parking lot.*

Let me know when they get into the building and then head for a window at the back of the building. Sen, go to that window too and join Zephyr.

What about you?

I'll come to you as quickly as I can.

I glanced at the agent while waiting for the computer and noticed he had gotten one arm free. I strode back two steps and shot him.

He slumped, out cold. I ran back to the computer and copied the last of the files before heading out of the office and toward Zephyr.

Hurry, he said, *they're in the building.*

A fraction of a second later, I heard a glass window blow out, and I ran toward it as Zephyr moved out of it, hopefully flying well enough.

Get in the air and away where you can't be seen. I ran around the corridor, powering myself faster and jumping through the gap in the window as men came up the stairs and shot in my direction.

Bullets pinged off the scale armor I was wearing, making me grateful it was tougher than the Kevlar I had been wearing. Although Kevlar stopped the bullets, there was enough of a resultant impact that I was usually knocked off my feet, and I would have been propelled into jagged glass had the dragon scales done the same.

As it was, I came away with only a small scratch from my own wobble as I'd jumped. Powering up toward Zephyr, I deliberately blasted air back into the building, intending to make it hard for them to get close and shoot at us.

It was only as I rose into the sky that I remembered the tranquilizer ammo we'd wanted to go back for.

I've got it, Zephyr said as he slowed and waited for me to catch up with him. Sen was curled up into his makeshift jacket, only her mushroom top poking out.

The compound grew smaller and farther away as we continued to head west for a while before turning north and back toward the cave. We'd managed to get the information, but we'd been seen doing it.

It was progress, but I had a sinking feeling we'd drawn the agents right to us again.

CHAPTER FOURTEEN

We landed by the entrance to the cave, right in the gully, and Zephyr sagged. I used my powers to steady him, and we moved behind the moss and into our makeshift home.

That really is exhausting, isn't it? Zephyr said as he sank to a sitting position. I pulled out the food we'd liberated, and we shared it with Sen and stuffed our faces. Not long after, I went to tend our plants and harvest what was ready.

I let most of the beans go to seed, thinking I'd need them to help defend us instead of eat, but I harvested more potatoes, carrots, tomatoes, and even some strawberries. The corn needed longer.

It was strange to grow so many different plants so quickly, but I didn't plant any replacements yet. Until we knew if the agents were going to find us, I wasn't taking a chance that my energy would be wasted.

I went back to Zephyr and Sen. The small myconid was keeping a lookout by the base of a cactus near the top of the gully.

Giving her some water and a pile of strawberries to eat,

I took the rest down to the cave and we set a small fire in the back of the cave and heated water to make stew. It didn't have any meat in it, but it still tasted good.

As Zephyr and I sat beside each other and ate, I found myself wishing he could turn back into a dragon again, and yet at the same time, I liked how it felt to have his arms around me and have a shoulder for me to rest my head on. However, I also liked how safe I felt when I was beside the large dragon.

I should be able to turn back soon. The process is complicated, but I think I almost got it the last time, he said, reading my thoughts. *Don't worry, I'm not rushing anything with you.*

My cheeks flushed at the last part. I couldn't remember feeling so unsure about a relationship before. I'd always been fairly confident, even as a teenager. But Zephyr was different.

Although I'd raised him, because of his memories and the genetic differences, he felt older than me. He had a maturity about him that a human of the equivalent age wouldn't have. It was strange, but I'd had him in my head for so long it felt so comfortable and right.

We knew so much about each other and could hide so little that being together made sense in so many ways. I loved him. But until the last twenty-four hours, being attracted to him hadn't been part of the equation. Now it was.

I leaned into him and inhaled, picking up on a scent I recognized. Even in human form, he smelled like Zephyr, and it helped me relax. A moment later, he leaned down and pressed his lips to mine.

It startled me, but I didn't pull away until he did.

Sorry, he said into my head. *I've always wondered what that would be like.*

Did it live up to your expectations? I asked

Let me check. He smirked and kissed me again, this time taking even longer.

No. It didn't. It was even better, he said, his voice almost a whisper.

I sighed and leaned into him until a squeak of surprise came from Sen.

Sen see people, she said, projecting what she could see toward us.

Shitsticks.

We had agents looking for us, a group of them fanning out and using flashlights to check out the area. Each of them was wearing a bulletproof vest and a gas mask and carried an assault rifle. With them were several dogs. While we watched, the canines picked up our scent and started barking.

Get the pack, and I'll get the ammo and other supplies, Zephyr said.

Sen, come down to us, I added, already doing as he suggested.

Zephyr grabbed the ammo crate and the new guns and pulled his heatproof cape around all of it. I yanked mine back on and then stuffed as much as I could into the pack while using my abilities to pull the rest closer.

Come on, Aella, he said, his voice sounding panicked as he ran to the entrance of our cave.

Get into the air. It's more important they don't see you like this than it is for me to get out without being seen.

I did a quick sweep of the cave, using the air to feel for

objects I might have missed, and then hurried after him. Sen bounded onto my shoulder, and I helped her slip into her usual hiding place in my jacket before blasting into the air outside the cave entrance.

Although I couldn't see Zephyr, I could feel him in the air above me, and I moved nearby, making sure not to get too close to him in case I was spotted. I didn't want them to know he was with me if it could be helped. No one at the base had seen him in human form, as far as we were aware. I planned to keep it that way.

Thankfully, the dogs kept the agents from looking up often as they all raced toward the cave and we flew away.

We headed farther east without thinking about our direction. There wasn't much left of the night, and we were going to need to find somewhere soon.

Once the agents were far behind us, I moved closer to Zephyr, not wanting to be away from him. I took over the task of holding the ammo box so he could focus on flying.

As far as I could tell, Zephyr didn't have the stamina I did when it came to using the air and magic to do anything. I thought that could be because it was an ability he had thanks to our bond, and not all of my power made it through the connection.

I had no idea if that was how it worked or not, but it was a theory, and it explained why he was struggling with having the same amount of energy and capacity.

After about an hour of flying east and a little north, steering clear of major population centers, we flew a little lower and found a quiet place to land for a moment.

We desperately needed to trim down what we were carrying again, and I needed to communicate with Erlan and the others. I reached into my pack and pulled out my communication stone.

Sen moved a little way off to keep watch while we settled into the bottom of what looked to be an abandoned quarry and I activated the stone. Almost immediately, Zephyr and I found ourselves in a darkened room, Zephyr looking like a dragon, much to our surprise.

It took less than a second for Ronan to appear, with Erlan beside him.

"Did you get the information?" Erlan asked before anyone else could speak.

I nodded but I frowned.

"It did not go as well as you hoped it would?" Ronan questioned, his gentle but deep melodic voice holding no judgment for the failure.

"The agents saw us, and they found our cave. We had to fly. I left more than a few seeds and plants behind," I said.

"I thought that might happen." Erlan didn't look put out by the news at all. "I've found somewhere you can stay for a while. It's directly north of the cave, on the edge of the Rockies near the Canadian border. There are cabins in the woods up there. There's a bunch that are often empty at this time of year. Mostly holiday retreats."

I blinked, wondering how he'd worked that out.

"There's one that the owners have left recently, and you should be able to borrow it without being worried they'll be coming back. You'll have to get Zephyr in the back doors and he'll have to sleep downstairs, but—"

"I'm sure we can handle getting Zephyr inside," I replied, cutting Erlan off but trying not to be irritated or short with him. It wasn't his fault we needed a new hideout.

"When you get there, communicate with me again, and I'll set up a direct VPN between the two places so you can transfer me the data and I can narrow down where Jacobs is."

I nodded and waited for Erlan to give me the exact address. When we told him where we were, he gave us the basic directions. I didn't understand them all, but Zephyr said he did, and then Erlan slipped out of the strange conversation and the dream-like room we were in.

"Is the Sanctuary safe?" I asked Ronan.

"Yes. The agents seem to have grown bored of looking for us, although I was worried they would begin trying again in the last day or so. Your sighting has refocused their attention away from us again."

"I'm glad being seen could aid you," I replied, my gratitude genuine.

"I will not deny feeling similarly, but I still hope for a day when such things are unnecessary."

"As do I, my friend. As do I. With any luck, it is coming."

The centaur bowed and cut the communication, returning his mind to the Sanctuary while we slipped back to the abandoned quarry.

With the fresh directions and purpose, we quickly ate and then got back in the air again. It was still a fair way to fly, and I knew we weren't going to be arriving during the night if we made the journey in one, but we had to try to get there swiftly without being seen.

I tried not to think about it too much, not wanting to worry.

I missed the warehouse and our friends. By now, I'd normally have gone to Minsheng and asked him about the best course of action, but I couldn't easily contact the Shishou or any of the others with him.

Although we'd flown at night many times, it felt strange this time. We were hiding in a way we'd never needed to before. The last time, we'd had to sneak, but we hadn't been worried about someone seeing us. Most people gave us space and simply stared if they realized who we were. Now we were wanted fugitives, and that meant every person was a threat.

We kept high enough that we wouldn't be seen until the sky started to brighten, then we took the opposite approach, flying low above the forest to minimize people being able to spot us from a distance. While over the trees, we kept away from major paths and tried not to worry too much, but we occasionally found ourselves out in the open, flying across plains, marshes, or rivers.

When the sun was about to rise and we were in yet another open space, I landed in a farmer's field and hunkered down below the level of the crops. We wouldn't be able to stay there for long, but we'd been up for a long time, and we'd both pushed ourselves.

Zephyr lay down beside me. I could feel he was more tired than I was. Sen hopped down and stuck her roots in the ground.

None of us spoke. There wasn't a lot to say. We were on the run, and we needed to both keep going and not be seen. It was an almost impossible situation.

Sleep, I said to Zephyr when I noticed him fighting his eyes closing. I hadn't asked him when he'd given up on sleeping the night before while he was working out how to take human form. There was a good chance that he hadn't had enough sleep for a while.

While I was also tired, I knew I could stay awake a little longer, especially as the sun rose in the sky. The cornfield was chilly, the ground cold and the plants offering little protection from the elements. It would aid me in staying awake.

Zephyr tried to protest, moving as if he intended to swap places with me, but I wouldn't let him and pushed him down to rest his head on my lap. For now, he could sleep and I would keep watch.

I felt the crops and air around me, not trying to control them but feeling it move as the wind rippled over the field.

The day dawned bright but colder than I was used to. We'd come a long way north and I felt the chill, especially since I was still wearing the heatproof jacket and pants.

We stayed like that for several hours, with nothing but animals disturbing the area around us. Now and then, cars passed on a small road, but it wasn't traveled frequently, and no one stopped or got any closer.

Sen also dozed, her roots drinking in whatever she needed.

While Zephyr slept, I nibbled on my share of the last of the food we had and took stock of the seeds and supplies we had left. The ammo had been a huge boost, and it made me feel more confident that some parts of the plan might work. We still needed one thing, however. We needed to find Jacobs, and soon.

As the sun rose higher, the clouds obscured it as they rolled in from the west. I felt myself growing sleepy. I'd been awake for a long time, and sitting there doing nothing wasn't helping.

I fought it, determined to give Zephyr as long as possible. When I'd been considering waking Zephyr for several minutes already, trying to hang on until he'd had three hours, he stirred naturally and opened his eyes.

He sat up. *Your turn. Then we'll get moving again.*

Are you sure?

I can feel how tired you are. Rest.

Not taking no for an answer, Zephyr shifted and pulled me so I was lying against him as he had been on me. Almost immediately my eyes closed and I finally stopped fighting.

My last thought was how grateful I was for Zephyr.

CHAPTER FIFTEEN

The sun was past the highest peak by the time I woke again. I was right where I'd fallen asleep, Zephyr's body close and warm. At some point, he'd slipped my jacket off and wrapped the blanket over us, our bodies keeping each other warm beneath it. It was a good way to wake up.

As I stirred, I looked up at him. He smiled and then kissed me, lingering with his lips against mine.

"That's going to take some getting used to," I said as he pulled back.

"I'm looking forward to getting you used to it," he replied, then offered me a drink.

It was strange to talk aloud, but it felt right while he was in human form.

While I drank, I noticed my stomach was empty. I reached for the nearest corn plant. I encouraged it to grow and ripen, the cobs already there just needing a little more length. When there were several good corn heads on the plant, I stopped. Zephyr reached for them and broke them off the plant.

I opened our pack, and he stuffed them inside. They would go with dinner later, assuming we could find anything else. I tried not to think about how Zephyr could have hunted us an animal if he was in dragon form and instead reached for the air again to see if anyone was nearby.

We were alone as far as I could tell. I motioned for Sen to join us. The dryad pulled up her roots and shook the dirt off them. She jumped onto my shoulder, leaving a couple of muddy footprints on my t-shirt.

While the sun was up and we could be seen, neither of us bothered to put our special clothing back on. If agents wanted to track us, there was no way we could easily stop them right now.

It was tempting to stay where we were. After all, we'd been there all day without trouble so far, but we were still a fair way off from the cabin Erlan had given us directions to, and I didn't want to have to fly through more of the night than we had to.

That meant walking looking like a couple of hikers. I put my cap on again and pulled my hair back into a ponytail, grateful no one knew what Zephyr looked like yet.

We walked for what felt like ages, going from one field to another, sticking to the edges or where there were already paths. Eventually, we came across a hiking trail that went into a large forest, a small car park showing us that several others would be in there too.

There was a small souvenir hut, but before I could head toward it to get more food, Zephyr put an arm out.

No one knows my face, he said. *Let me go and buy what we need.*

I nodded and handed him some cash, giving him several twenties rather than anything larger. Better not to make the clerk suspicious.

Zephyr strolled inside and grabbed some bottles of water from a cabinet by the door before going deeper where I couldn't see him. I tried not to appear to be fretting and encouraged Sen to tuck herself into the top of the pack in case another car pulled in while I was waiting.

Thankfully Zephyr didn't take too long, even if every second dragged.

When he reappeared, I noticed that he was carrying a couple of items I hadn't expected.

Map, he said, handing me a brochure. *And sunglasses.*

He had two pairs and put one of them on me.

Makes it harder for people to recognize you.

Good call, I replied as we loaded the water bottles into the pack's side pockets except for one he kept and put the sandwiches, chips, fruit, and candy bars in the pack.

Once more, I felt weighed down, but Zephyr took it off me and slung it on his own back.

I think in human culture, it's supposed to be me carrying heavy things, is it not?

I chuckled as I nodded. If he wanted to carry all the stuff for a bit, I had no objection.

Not sure what else to do, I slipped my hand into his like a normal couple might, and with our map and a decently marked trail, we set off. The forest trail was supposed to encompass several loops and bring us back to where we started, but on the far end of the section of forest was a trail that was marked as a path that hikers on a multi-day hike could take.

It had bear warnings and various other information on it, but none of that would matter. When you had faced an entire army of soldiers with heavy weaponry and tanks, a single bear wasn't much of a threat.

We walked along in silence for a while. The forest was peaceful. For a moment, I could almost forget we were on the run and pretend this was a lovely day trip or date for the two of us. That we weren't in danger, and this was just somewhere we could hide.

If I'd been more of a nature person it probably would have been better, but even I could appreciate the beauty we were surrounded by.

More than once we saw animals. Several deer made an appearance, and we saw a few strange-looking birds I'd never seen before.

We heard some people in the distance at one point, but wherever they were on the trails, we didn't bump into them. Their voices came from the left of the path. The map showed there was a small campsite in that direction when I consulted it.

Passing by the turnoff to the campsite, we walked until I was footsore and I was pretty sure Zephyr was the same.

When his stomach let out a loud rumble, we stopped to eat and rest, walking off the path a few feet first and hiding in case anyone else came along while we were eating.

We shared out what we had. We didn't consume anything Zephyr hadn't just bought, but we hadn't needed to use our powers most of the day and we were still hidden, so I considered it a win.

During the afternoon we'd drunk most of the water, but

we had enough left. I was pretty sure we'd get where we needed to go without needing to restock.

We ate fast despite being tired. Our bodies would get rest once we were flying again. We continued traveling north, each step awkward and achy after getting to sit down for a while.

The forest darkened fast as the sun set, and more of the wildlife grew brave enough to roam. The trail became harder to follow, no longer anything more than a hiker's trail from one campsite to another. Still we trudged on, needing it darker than this to be able to get into the air without being seen against the sky.

Sen had curled up in the pack again and gone to sleep by the time it was dark enough. We had been going slowly for the last hour or so. Zephyr led the way, able to see far better than I could, even with my elven eyesight.

Finally, we felt safe enough to fly again, and I took the pack back. We lifted off the ground together and were soon above the trees. Wrapped in the strange material Chris had made us once more, I felt instantly cold.

We shifted our direction slightly, the trail having taken us a little too far east, then we flew on, eating up the miles far quicker than our legs could.

It still took several hours, but the clouds in the sky continued to thicken and thankfully hid the moon.

Zephyr flew ahead of us, his sense of direction better than mine. We avoided major towns and cities, not wanting to risk being seen by so many more observant eyes, but eventually, the mountains rose ahead of us again, and Zephyr went lower to identify where we needed to go.

We had to land just outside the next town we saw and check the name.

We've got about another twenty miles to go, Zephyr said as he pushed up into the air again.

I exhaled, relief washing over me. I still had the energy to fly farther than that, but we'd done a lot of flying in the last few days, and I was more than tired of it.

Although I loved flying in general, it had become too much of a good thing. I was ready to land and do something normal for a few days.

The small village by the cabins soon came into view and we landed again, staying out of the light and looking for a road sign to help us find our bearings.

It took a while to find it. We flew along above a dirt track. Most of the cabins were dark, the people occupying them asleep, but we saw a couple with the lights obscured by blinds or curtains and one with a porch light revealing a large red truck and a dog kennel.

We rose higher, hoping not to alarm the canine within, and I was angry the owner had left it out in the cold. Some humans sucked.

Finally, Zephyr spotted the cabin Erlan had told us to head to. We touched down in the backyard, hoping not to be seen by anyone. It was a stunning wood structure and I imagined us living somewhere like it more permanently, but I was taken out of the happy daydream by Zephyr trying the back door and finding it locked.

I frowned. None of us had thought about getting into the cabin when it didn't belong to us. There was a keyhole, but I wasn't sure I wanted to pick the lock if there was an easier alternative.

Zephyr looked around, spotted a plant pot, and shifted it. He picked up a key, and I had to stifle a laugh. Why were people so predictable?

Within seconds we were inside, and I'd found a switch to bathe the kitchen in light.

It was spacious, clean, and well-kept. I took my boots off by the door, not wanting to track mud through, then went to see if there was anything in the place.

I noticed a freezer inside the pantry, whirring to show it was on. Opening it revealed a bunch of meat, cartons of ice cream, some frozen veggies, a few frozen microwave meals, and a number of frozen pizzas.

Grabbing a few of the latter, I held them up with a grin on my face.

Hungry? I asked Zephyr.

Now they were worth flying here for, he replied, going to the oven and turning it on.

It felt weird to see him moving about a kitchen and helping me prepare dinner, but it was also nice. While the pizzas were cooking, we explored the rest of the cabin. There were four bedrooms, all of them under the pitched roof. There was also a good-sized sitting room, a small library and office combined, and a garage.

The place was perfect for our needs, and it made me very grateful for Erlan's research and how he'd found it for us.

After we'd eaten, I considered using the communication stone to let Ronan and the others know we'd made it there okay, but I noticed the time and stopped myself. It was the early hours of the morning.

Instead, we found Sen a glass of water, and Zephyr took

my hand before leading me to the master bedroom. It felt strange to be heading to a bed with him.

As Zephyr had grown, we'd made a custom area at the warehouse, and we slept on the floor pretty much everywhere else, but now we could use a normal bed again. It was only when Zephyr walked through the door that I understood how much easier it was for him.

No more not fitting through doors, I said, grinning.

And no more being left out in the rain or somewhere you're not.

We didn't shut the door with only Sen in the house, but it wasn't weird. I just hoped no one came while we were there. Sen was downstairs to give us early warning.

At first, I wasn't sure what to do. I hesitated to take my clothing off.

I've seen it all before, Zephyr pointed out. *You've had me in the shower with you.*

Before I knew you could take human form.

True, but I've still seen everything.

The knowledge made my cheeks heat. I'd forgotten that, and I'd stopped doing it when he'd gotten bigger.

Zephyr came over to me, wearing nothing but his pants. He took my hands in his, his gaze meeting mine.

Nothing needs to happen between us until you're ready. Just make yourself comfy and join me in the bed. We'll snuggle like we usually do, and when we're more used to it, we'll come back to the possibilities we now have.

I nodded and smiled at him. He let go of me and got into the bed, deliberately looking away.

I took off my pants and removed my bra, taking my time to slip the straps down under my sleeves and unhooking the back so I could pull it out from underneath without removing my shirt. Then I pulled back the covers and got in with him.

He turned and slipped his arm around me to encourage me to come closer, and I didn't refuse. Inhaling and breathing in his familiar scent helped me relax. It was Zephyr, and I'd been sleeping beside him for the best part of two years.

Closing my eyes, I settled down to get some sleep in a decent bed again.

CHAPTER SIXTEEN

I woke up close to Zephyr, although I noticed his pants were gone, only boxers covering his skin. It was a little strange to see his bare chest. I almost shifted away as he stirred, but I found I didn't want to.

He woke up a few minutes later and smiled at me.

I like waking up with you, he said.

Me too, I replied, reaching for Sen to check she was nearby.

During the night, she'd moved to a new position near the top of the stairs.

Sen hear noise, she said a moment later.

I sat up, and so did Zephyr. However, before we could do anything else, the back door opened and footsteps came inside.

Shitsticks, I thought as I dived off the bed to grab my pants. Beside me, Zephyr did the same, both of us pulling them on as whoever was coming in moved through to the sitting room.

"They're here," a familiar voice said, making me exhale and relax. "I recognize Aella's pack."

"We're up here," I called to Minsheng. "We'll be down in a minute or two. Just let me get dressed."

There were more shuffling footsteps, and someone put something heavy down. I glanced at Zephyr as he put his shirt back on, and I tried to make myself presentable.

They were in for a huge surprise.

Ready before me, Zephyr made his way to the door as someone started coming up the stairs. He pulled the door closed as he slipped out of the room to give me some privacy, and I heard Minsheng gasp.

"Zephyr, is that you?" he asked.

"I know. It's strange. I think I'm stuck like this for now."

There was silence. I considered going to see his reaction, but it was funnier to listen while I brushed my hair.

"Wow, it's... I never... I thought we'd see you do it, or you'd still have some more obvious signs, but it's just your eyes."

There was a moment of silence, and again I almost left the room to join them, but then I heard Minsheng shift.

"Are you... Were you and Aella in the master bedroom together?"

"Of course," Zephyr replied. I paused on the other side of the door.

There was another awkward silence.

"Be careful with her. I know you're bonded, and I can't imagine what that's like, but she doesn't need a horny dragon getting used to being human taking advantage of that. She—"

"I know you're being protective of her and think you

are helping," Zephyr replied, interrupting Minsheng. "But don't. I wouldn't ever do anything to hurt her. I *can't* do anything to hurt her. But if anything did happen between us it would be none of your business. She's a grown woman who has been through hell and back and is hated by many just for being herself."

"Of course she's very capable. I care about her," Minsheng said, his voice even quieter.

"I care about her too. Trust her, even if you don't trust me."

I heard Zephyr stride past Minsheng and down the stairs, his bare feet padding on the wood. More than a little angry at how Minsheng had just talked to Zephyr, I yanked the door open and glared at my Shishou. He had his arm raised as if he was about to knock on the door, but he lowered it quickly.

"How dare you! That's Zephyr you just said that crap to. He's been in battle with me. Put his life on the line to keep all of us safe, and not once left my side unless he had to. We've been together every moment since my life was turned upside down, trained together, and he even went to prison with me when he didn't have to. He's still that Zephyr, even if he's now in a male human skin."

"I know—"

"I don't think you do," I cut in. "Not all men deserve to be treated as if they can't keep it in their pants just because a few can't. He's a good dragon and a good man."

Minsheng raised his hands in a defensive position but I couldn't stop glaring at him and shaking. Zephyr and Sen were everything to me. We were in each other's heads. We were always there for each other, and not once had

Zephyr tried to get me to give him something I didn't want to.

"I'm sorry," Minsheng said after a while, deflating as he did. "You're right. I judged. I just saw him coming out of the room as a man, and I immediately jumped into over-protective father mode. But you're right. He's still Zephyr, even if seeing him in human form is strange. He deserves more respect. You deserve more respect, too."

I nodded, the apology helping to calm me and make me relax.

Exhaling, I reached for Sen. The myconid was sitting on the top step to one side. She jumped up onto my shoulder, looking between Minsheng and me as she did.

"We've got some news for you," he said a moment later.

I didn't respond, hearing the others react to Zephyr and wanting to make sure no one else gave him any trouble. Slipping my hand into his as soon as I reached his side, I made my feelings of support clear.

"This is so cool," Erlan said as he came forward, Newton on his shoulder.

I smiled, grateful for the happier reaction.

"We'd like to keep this fairly quiet, to begin with," Zephyr replied. "At the moment, you are the only people who know I can do this."

Behind Erlan stood Chris. I nodded in his direction as he leaned against the doorjamb.

"Secret's safe with me," he replied. "Only people I talk to these days are all right here or back in the warehouse. I'm just excited to be out of the house. Also, I brought you a gift."

In his hands was a very modern bow and a quiver of strange-looking arrows.

"Did you make these?" I asked as I moved closer to take them.

"Not exactly. I had a hand in the design, and the organization made them a reality. Should have done it before now, but, well, better late than never."

I looked inside the quiver and noticed that not all of the arrows were the same.

"Some of them contain Zephyr's breath weapon, others smoke, some are tasers, and others are explosive. They're color-coded, but most importantly, they're weighted the same, and the organization provided some practice ones of a similar weight and design to help you get used to them."

The revelation made me blink, but then a grin spread across my face. We might have taken all the tranquilizer ammo, but now I had something even cooler to go with it.

"Ronan approved. Said it was far better than a gun," Erlan added. "No one has made me one yet, though."

"If I find it useful and can provide a good tactical reason, I'm sure I can twist their arm to get you one as well," I replied. "Imagine if yours were full of something flammable."

"Oh, I have been." He broke into a broad grin, and I felt better. These were my people, and I was grateful they'd come to help.

Before I could ask how the others were doing, Daisy came in through the back door.

"Car is stashed out of the way," she said before she saw Zephyr and me.

She squealed and came running over, the first to understand that Zephyr was Zephyr.

"Oh, my, you're handsome as a human, aren't you?" She grinned and hugged him. He squeezed her back, then we were all hugging and greeting each other.

I was pretty sure I heard Minsheng apologize to Zephyr.

"So, what's the news?" I asked, looking at my Shishou.

"Well, we think we've found Jacobs. But..."

"Spit it out," I said as I sat down, trying to not sound as anxious to know as I was and failing miserably.

"He's not going to be easy to reach, and I'm not sure our idea of getting him to stop will work." Minsheng looked at Chris and Erlan, and we moved as one to the table while Minsheng and Daisy prepared breakfast.

"I found more than just his location," Erlan said as he flipped open his laptop. "He works at a base on the East Coast, not far from Washington, DC. I'm pretty sure he reports straight to the President."

I raised my eyebrows. I'd expected him to be someone high up, but not *that* high up. Did that mean that all the Presidents in the past had been sitting on the knowledge that mythicals existed and the government had been keeping them quiet?

"I found documents that suggest Jacobs hates our kind. Apparently, he ran into a group of elves as a kid, and they were...less than pleasant. Some young part-elves with powers who didn't have the sense not to use them on a human," Erlan continued.

"So now he hates every elf out there because he thinks we're all bullies."

"Something like that. I don't think you're going to be able to change his mind."

"We were never sure we could," I replied, reaching for Zephyr again and squeezing his hand.

It felt as if our situation was getting even less hopeful. We'd come so far, but not far enough.

"What about the President?" I asked a moment later. "What does he get told?"

"We don't know exactly. I'm not sure it's the whole truth," Chris added, implying he'd been helping with the research. "The whole agency was given a code name a while back. It gets funding, and it's questioned now and then by Congress, but that's very different from the information someone might be handing the top man."

"Okay, focus on that for now," I said. "I want to know what he thinks of us and what Jacobs tells the person he answers to. In the meantime, we'll have to do what we can to come up with a new plan."

It sounds like it would be useful if I could turn into a dragon again, Zephyr said.

What makes you say that? I replied, finally feeling more comfortable with him as a human.

If we're going to have to take on Jacobs another way, being a dragon would benefit us after all.

Maybe. Want to go for a walk now?

In daylight?

There's not much daylight left, and we'll be careful. No one knows you're not human. I'm the only person they might recognize. I can wear those sunglasses you bought me yesterday.

Zephyr hesitated another moment, then agreed to go for a walk once we'd eaten.

It made me feel a little better. I knew that after losing Lorcan, I couldn't ask any of the others to risk their lives on a mission against a man who was comfortable seeing people like us die. Even though Erlan was also a mythical, he'd been safe in the Sanctuary until we'd come along.

In a lot of ways, dealing with Jacobs was unfinished business for Zephyr and me. We had started this whole thing. Our path had been set when I'd found Zephyr's egg. I was pretty sure he wouldn't have hatched if I hadn't found it and picked it up.

However, the more I heard, the more the problem seemed to lie with Jacobs. He had ordered Crawley and Knox around to the point Crawley had betrayed the agency she'd dedicated her life to and Knox had died, his desire for revenge going beyond his respect for what we wanted.

Both of them had been answering to Jacobs. But did he truly answer to anyone?

After pulling on a sweatshirt and finding another hat, I donned the sunglasses Zephyr had bought me. He did the same to cover his purple eyes, and we strode out the back of the cabin, doing our best to look like a normal couple on a walk together.

While we walked, we talked in our heads, working out what to do about Jacobs. I felt as if we were right back to square one again, but farther from all our friends, the Sanctuary, and everything else that mattered to us.

Leaving the country is still an option, Zephyr pointed out after a little while.

Maybe, but everyone we know is here.

They are, but the organization appears to be willing to help us, he added. *There are bound to be mythicals in other countries, too.*

I nodded, knowing he was right, but the rest of the world had been very quiet on the subject.

We walked down the rest of the hill in silence, and I considered if we could simply start again somewhere else. We could easily hop a border into another country. Canada and Mexico were easily accessible. We could possibly even continue, going from Alaska to Russia, then to Greenland, Iceland, or even farther. Possibly to the UK.

For a moment, I indulged in the idea of starting again with Zephyr in Scotland. It was supposed to be a beautiful country and the British were far more practical about everything. As long as we didn't kill anyone, they were likely to leave us alone.

There's a chance the US would insist on getting us back, Zephyr said a little while later, interrupting my daydream about the idea of meeting the Queen.

We continued to walk, thinking seriously once more.

As we reached the edge of the village at the foot of the hill, we noticed a small convenience store. I considered going in, but I didn't want to draw too much attention to us. There was always a chance that someone would recognize me, and I wasn't taking that chance today.

When we turned the next corner, however, I wished we had. We almost smacked straight into a pair of agents, the two of them carrying a crate between them.

It contained a cat-like creature I'd seen an example of once before—a sphinx. The agents were pulling a cloth over the cage to hide it from prying eyes, but I'd seen everything I needed to.

With a deft flick of air, I knocked them both off their feet and lifted the cage they were about to drop. I carefully guided it to the ground, the creature yowling the entire time.

Zephyr bent down and opened the cage, yanking the door open with such strength it snapped entirely. The creature flew out of the cage and ran up the road.

The agents got to their feet, pulling their guns. I was pretty sure they recognized us. Their body language was aggressive.

While I reached for my dart gun, I used my air abilities to blow them back again and knocked the guns out of their hands. At the same time, I grew the nearby weeds and used them to hold the agents' limbs in place. Then I shot them both with tranquilizer darts.

What now? Zephyr asked, looking around. There were two civilians farther down the same street.

I looked around for the agents' car and soon spotted it. I used my abilities to lift the agents and carry them over to it. Zephyr found the keys in one of the agents' pockets. He used them to open the door, and I placed the two agents inside. With that done, I shut the door and locked it from the inside.

While I was doing the last part, Zephyr went back over to the cage and picked it up. The sphinx was long gone, but we weren't leaving the cage to make it easy for the agents to recapture it.

We should go back to the cabin. We've blown our cover.

I sighed as Zephyr looked at me. That hadn't lasted long.

CHAPTER SEVENTEEN

It didn't take long to get back up the hill with me using my abilities to help us avoid feeling fatigued. Zephyr also practiced similarly, finally getting used to doing everything I did.

Sen remained in her usual place in my jacket. The myconid was put out by so much strangeness and moving from place to place. She wasn't getting to stretch her legs much while we were trying to be so discreet.

The moment we arrived back, Minsheng leapt up from the table.

"It's on social media already," he said. "No footage, but there's a photo of you putting an agent into the car."

I exhaled. Of course there was. Everything was put up on the internet these days.

"They don't know exactly where you are, so we've got some time," my Shishou continued, "but we probably shouldn't stay another night."

"Okay," I said, already having realized this. We needed to go somewhere else. I just wasn't sure where.

"What else did you find on Jacobs?" I asked Erlan as he came into the room, laptop in hand.

We spent the next hour going through everything, mostly skim-reading briefing reports. I didn't know how Erlan had managed to obtain the classified information, but I was impressed.

"Chris helped," Erlan said when Zephyr asked him about it. "He has some interesting friends, and the gnomes have some interesting magic available to them."

There wasn't a lot of time. It looked as if we were going to have to work with what we had. I was grateful for my team and more than a little relieved. I didn't have everything I needed to sort this whole thing out, but I hoped it would all fall into place as we went.

"All right," I said as yet another fighter jet passed overhead. "Get back to the car and head back to the Sanctuary. Zephyr, Sen, and I will handle this from here. Zephyr knows another place we can lie low near Jacobs. We'll only need another night or two," I said, processing out loud as much as telling them what would happen.

Minsheng and Daisy immediately pulled me into a hug, almost crushing Sen.

"It feels wrong sending you into this alone," he said.

"I know. I miss you all, but they're trying to make out that I'm leading you all into trouble, and they're constantly targeting the three of us. We need to do this next bit alone and make sure they don't judge any of you as participants."

I went to the freezer and started restocking my pack, grateful whoever owned the place had left it well stocked.

I then found some notepaper and a pen, wrote them a note and apologized, and left a stack of cash to cover the cost of everything we'd used, plus a little extra. I tucked it in the freezer so it wasn't visible from a window and ushered everyone else out.

It was getting darker, but I was loath to fly while it was still so easy to see us.

We can fly out of trouble quickly. Let's wait a little longer, Zephyr said. He slipped his hand into mine as he spoke, and I felt a little better.

I have a feeling that my dragon abilities are going to be more useful in the next few days, he added.

I think so too, I replied.

Not sure what else to say or do, I went over everything in the pack again. I didn't want to pressure him when he was stuck, and I liked having him as a human. However, the dragon was what we needed, and that meant he needed to find a way to turn back.

If we were going to fly all the way to Jacobs' location, then we needed to have Zephyr able to carry me while I rested and ate, and I needed to help him to go faster than either of us was capable of flying alone.

On top of that, we needed his breath weapon if we were going to achieve our goal without killing anyone. There weren't enough darts in the small case of ammo we'd taken, nor could I shoot people fast enough.

No sooner had I thought this than I felt something happen in my awareness of Zephyr. He was always in the back of my mind, even when I wasn't looking at him. The bond between us never went away, but I'd grown so used to it that it felt strange to have it change.

I whipped around to see a dragon standing in the back garden. *My dragon*. I rushed to him and exhaled with relief.

There. I don't think it will be so hard to change again in the future, but it's not easy. I can't do it often. At least, not yet.

I encouraged him to unfurl his wings, curious how they would look and whether they had healed while he wasn't using them. Whatever magic enabled Zephyr to take human form gave his dragon body the ability to regenerate.

His wings still had holes in them, but they were smaller and looked healthier, the edges less tattered. It gave me hope that one day he'd be back to normal, especially since I noticed some older small holes that had been taking forever to heal were either gone entirely now or also a lot smaller.

It's not perfect yet, he said a moment later. *But I think more time as a human should solve the problem.*

This is good enough for now. I hugged his leg, unable to hug more than that of him in this form, and he chuckled. Sen bounded up onto his back, and I grabbed the pack from the kitchen.

We didn't need to fly yet. The skies were quiet, but I considered zipping up for a moment to see what we might be able to see.

They're likely to be looking for us. It's better if we keep watch and fly as soon as it's dark or as we see a sign of the agents.

I frowned, not liking the idea of waiting for an unknown threat to come find us, but equally unable to disagree. He was right, we needed to hang on for a dark sky so we wouldn't show up.

If Jacobs knew we were coming, it would wreck our plan. If nothing else, he could go elsewhere, and we'd have to find him all over again.

The minutes dragged by as I watched from the front window, my body almost entirely shielded by the partially drawn curtain. Up in the hills, we couldn't see any other cabins from our spot or be seen by anyone in them, but there was a dirt track that ran up the middle of the hill and I could see parts of this through gaps in the trees.

I nibbled on some cookies while I watched, feeding Sen and checking in on Zephyr with my mind so often he growled at me for bugging him.

I was so tense my muscles ached and my feet hurt, but I didn't stop watching.

Slowly, the sun sank and the hill and cabin grew darker, but still no trouble arrived. Although I wanted to reach out to the others and ask them if they were safely on their way back to the Sanctuary I didn't dare, even with the burner phone. I had to trust they could get themselves out of trouble if it came.

All four of them were used to dealing with the agency by now and had escaped from them more than once. It made me smile to think of some of the early ways we'd evaded the agents. How we'd dressed as cosplayers once, and how we'd had car chases. It had been a wild few years, but so far, we'd managed to keep going.

Holding onto that thought, I went over all the information we had in my head. It wasn't complete. Our plan had holes in it. Holes I still needed to fix if I could, but there was no way to be sure that something was the right course of action, and I was getting tired.

Despite us being used to being awake at night, I hadn't been sleeping anywhere near enough to cope with this much tension. We needed to go soon, or I was going to fall asleep where I stood.

I moved around, hoping that might help me wake up a bit. As I did, I noticed movement, and I froze again.

Soldiers were coming up the road, guns in hands, gas masks on, and dogs with them. The dogs were tracking our scent, and it made me more than a little angry that we hadn't thought of that.

Time to go, Zephyr said. I couldn't have agreed more with him. I ran to the back of the house and scooped Sen up as Zephyr leapt and unfurled his great wings.

Giving him a boost to get him into the air more swiftly, I powered myself up there with him and then onto his back. I wasn't wearing the heatproof clothing, and neither was he. We'd opted not to use it for a lot longer this time.

Although it aided us when we had someone on our tail or below us, it was less useful when we needed to fly long distances and people were less likely to be aiming weapons in our direction.

It also didn't give us any way to fool them into thinking we were going in a different direction.

The last few times we'd been hunted, we had flown opposite to our intended direction, landed when we'd lost the agents, and shrouded ourselves in the cloaks before continuing. We didn't plan to do that a third time.

They were unlikely to believe our misdirection this time. We were hoping that meant it made more sense to fly in the direction we were aiming for from the start.

Since we didn't plan on stopping anywhere for long, once we had lost the agents, we didn't need to worry as much. I was also tired of being so cold all the time while wearing them.

Admittedly, it would probably help keep me awake.

We were spotted while we were still getting into the air above the trees on the hillside. The night wasn't yet dark enough to hide us, and the dogs were already guiding the soldiers to the cabin we'd been in. With any luck, our scent trail would distract them from following that line of inquiry, and they'd ignore the house in their desire to follow us.

Either way, we didn't plan on making it easy for them to follow us. Zephyr quickly climbed high, and I blasted air down to meet the bullets and stop them from damaging his wings any further.

He still had enough holes in one that it wasn't giving him as much lift as the other, but I could help ease that pressure by controlling the airflow.

When the soldiers gave up firing, I came closer to him and checked over his back in the fading light. The scales on his back where the explosion had hit and tore some off were looking almost as good as new. There was just a little color difference left between the older scales and newer ones.

It won't hurt for you to ride me anymore. Don't worry, Zephyr said as the unmistakable sound of jet planes came closer.

I landed on his back, being more gentle than normal. I knew he was trying to encourage me, and there was no way for him to know for sure. Thankfully, he was right. I settled in my usual spot, and Sen tucked in against me.

Although it wasn't the perfect situation and we had an

incoming enemy, the whole world suddenly felt right again. Flying with Zephyr like this had become so normal I hadn't realized how much I needed it until it was gone, and now I was getting it back.

Exhaling with relief, I reached for the trees and had them trash the cars, the soldiers' weapons, and anything else they could get hold of. I did my best not to hurt anything but property and weaponry. It gave us the reprieve we needed from the ground forces as we banked east and picked up speed.

The jets were soon with us, coming up from behind. There were three of them, and they'd taken up a flight pattern. Now we needed to deal with them.

Pine cones, Zephyr suggested. *Grab some from the forest floor and pelt their engines with them.*

I lifted my eyebrows, wondering if it would work. Whenever we were up against jets or helicopters, I felt bad. There was no way to take their craft out of the sky without running the risk of killing the pilot.

Despite that fear, I did as he suggested. As much as I didn't want to hurt them, I wasn't going to let them stop us either. We had to swoop a little lower so my mind could find the pine-based missiles, but Zephyr performed amazingly, flying us above the trees while I gathered ammo and lifted it up to us.

Somewhere behind us, the jets opened fire. I blasted air back, but not before large bullets pinged off both my scale armor and Zephyr's hide.

Zephyr banked again, taking us outside of the attack zone and giving me the opportunity to do as he suggested. I hit the engine of the jet with over half the pine cones, hearing the loud noise as they were torn to shreds on the rotating blades but also hearing the engine change sound as pieces became lodged.

There was a spark as the flammable material built up enough to start a fire and blow the engine entirely.

I exhaled as the pilot ejected and the jet went down, a flaming ball coming out of the back. It plowed toward the houses below, and I panicked. There was no way I could let innocent people get hurt.

Instead of trying to defend us from the remaining jets or attack another, I concentrated all my abilities on slowing the jet and using a tree to reach up and wrap strong branches around each other to form a barrier.

The jet hit the tree with a loud crash, a crumple of metal, and a splinter of wood. Before I could stop it, the tree went over and landed on a garage and the car parked in front of it.

There was another crunch of metal, but I was pretty sure no one had been hurt.

As more bullets came toward us, Zephyr lifted up and flew closer to the forest again. We needed to get away from civilian areas. I exhaled and tried to calm my racing heart as the jets chased us down.

There were only two now, and although I could do the same with them, I wanted to make it harder for them to shoot us a lot sooner.

I'll take one, you take the other, Zephyr said. *I'll make sure I don't kill anyone.*

It was better than flying together and presenting one target, so I powered up and off him, drawing the fire as both jets targeted me over Zephyr. I almost grinned as the dragon dug his powerful claws into the back of the second jet. They were going to regret taking us on, even if they were just following orders.

A bunch more pine cones and some direct attacks from me as I landed on the back and dug in my knife, and my jet was also disabled. With a little help from Zephyr, I landed the two demolished jets: one in a clearing in the woods and the other in a dirt parking lot.

We came together again, and I rested for a moment on Zephyr's back.

You okay? I asked, checking he hadn't taken any more damage to his wings.

I'm good. Hopefully, now they'll leave us alone.

CHAPTER EIGHTEEN

Four hours later, I was falling asleep on Zephyr's back, my body hunkered down and Sen fast asleep in my jacket.

We'd finally put on the heatproof gear when we'd noticed more helicopters looking for us. It seemed they had every vehicle they had access to trying to work out where we had flown off to.

I'd eaten more snacks to keep my energy up, but it wasn't my abilities letting me down now so much as my lack of sleep.

Zephyr slipped down and landed by a barn at the edge of a field full of a crop I didn't recognize.

Rest here for a few hours. Nap, then we'll start again, he said.

But we shouldn't waste the dark.

No, but we'll be there soon. We're making good time now I can fly again. Please, sleep, and then we'll make the last leg.

Not sure I had the capacity to argue, I found some hay to lie down in and curled up. Zephyr sat down close by, but he kept his head turned toward the field and gazed along the horizon. With that the last image on my mind, I fell into the sweet oblivion of sleep.

Zephyr woke me a short while later, the sky almost as dark but contained a few more clouds.

Time to find Jacobs.

I nodded and quickly ate, offering something to Zephyr as well.

Don't worry about me. I've already deprived the farmer of some pigs. I don't think I'll need to eat for a while. He grinned, and I tried not to think about what that meant.

Of course, he needed to eat, and he was both fast enough and quiet enough that I didn't doubt he could easily hunt the slower-moving defenseless animals. I'd found it was best not to think too much about it beyond that.

After checking we had everything we needed for what was to come and that I'd stowed everything in the appropriate pockets and places, I let Zephyr know I was ready.

This would be the last leg of our journey. We would find Jacobs and finally end this once and for all.

It didn't take us long to get into the air and flying again. I used my abilities to help Zephyr, feeling his tiredness and trying to help him rest a little as well. Already I felt guilty that he hadn't had a proper rest when I'd done nothing but sleep, but he'd eaten, and that was an improvement on some of our journeys recently.

We swallowed up the miles, traveling across several more state boundaries. The cabin in the woods had been a fair way across the country, and we'd done nothing but travel east since. It was a lot of ground to cover, but we weren't too far from the East Coast now. Another few hours and we should be able to see the edge of the country.

The sun would be up before we got to Jacobs, but we were just going to have to deal with that when the time came.

I tensed as I heard yet more helicopters. They were flying in a search pattern, several of them fanned out in a group. Silently, Zephyr lifted higher until they were far below us. It made me wary. While I'd known they were likely to bring the army out against us, I hadn't expected this level of dedication.

It was possibly how well we kept evading them and that we'd attacked yet another of their compounds on our own. Could Jacobs know we were coming after him?

We just need to stick to the plan, Zephyr said. *It's a good one. Whatever happens, fleeing to Europe is always an option.*

I heard him chuckle, and it made me relax again. He was right. It wasn't funny, but he knew when to say everything. It made me adore him all the more.

With the helicopters behind us, we descended again, and I started to look for our target. Jacobs wasn't right on the East Coast, but he wasn't far off it. We needed to pay more attention to where we were going and what towns and cities were below us.

As the sun poked the first sliver above the horizon, Zephyr changed direction until we were heading northeast into the brightening morning. We could see the landmarks below us, and it made it easier to work out where we were.

I shivered a short while later, the clouds in the sky promising a wet and windy day.

Let's land and get these heatproof jackets back off, Zephyr said a moment later.

He dived down and landed by a lake and a large boatshed, and I set down beside him. It wasn't an ideal place to stop, but it was better than nothing, and the building was the largest for several miles.

I was pulling off my jacket when the sound of aircraft grew louder. Looking at Zephyr, I noticed he was already gazing in that direction. I didn't doubt he'd heard them before me, and that was the real reason he'd landed.

I helped him get out of the fabric and bundled it into the bag Chris had provided. Instead of putting the bag back on Zephyr's back, I broke the rusted lock on the boat yard's side door and wandered inside.

There were several boats in the water and I ran to the nearest one, a yacht with the main cabin door open. I hurried into it and looked for a storage cabinet.

After stuffing the bag into it and covering it with the ropes that had been inside, I hurried back to Zephyr's side. Sen had transferred to my pack to sleep some more, the small myconid knowing there wasn't a lot she could do to help right now.

There wasn't room for all of us in the boatshed, but I knew we were ready to keep going no matter how much attention we attracted. Ideally, we would make it hard for them to follow us or work out where we were going, but we'd gotten close to our goal and every mile we grew closer, the better our odds were of succeeding.

With that in mind, we got back into the air and lifted up high again. One of the helicopter pilots spotted us immediately. They all homed in on us, the line breaking to become a circle.

We were far more maneuverable, which gave us a clear advantage, but there were a lot more of them than normal today.

I tried not to worry about the details beyond our control and focused on the problem at hand. We needed to lose these guys. Or ground them. And we needed to do it fast.

Reaching out with my mind, I took control of the air and tried to kick up a storm. With the moist air in the area I had an easier time of it, but I didn't have the control or the time to create a twister before the helicopters started shooting.

Bullets hit Zephyr's scales, making him grunt and pull up again, pain flaring when they hit a more sensitive area.

Concerned about his wings, I gave up on the twister idea and focused on a single helicopter. I reached for the trees below and stripped them of fruits, nuts, and any other projectiles I could find. At the same time, I unslung the bow on my back and the new arrows Chris had given me.

While Zephyr dodged, I hit the first helicopter with whatever I'd pulled off the trees. I looked for the explosive arrows in my batch. I eventually found the marker that I thought Chris had said was explosive and then aimed at the closest helicopter while Zephyr flew up again, giving me the clearest shot he could.

Taking several deep breaths and concentrating, I shot at the back.

I hit the tail, and it exploded. The pilots were flung around, desperately trying to eject and forcing me to try to help them again if I didn't want them to die. I almost didn't when the rest of the flying nuisances around us opened fire again, but I powered up off Zephyr's back and did my best to help it land safely.

Go up and get east, I told Zephyr as some of them went after him. The rest turned their fire on me. *I'll catch up once we've dealt with a few.*

Panic filled me with so many airborne adversaries, but I was determined not to kill anyone. I flew lower and lower as I slowed the damaged helicopter and landed it.

As I was blasting back up again, several bullets hit the torso of my scaled armor. It knocked me back and into a tree. I smacked my head, seeing stars as I slid downward.

I hit the ground with a bump that rattled my bones and the helicopters continued to fire at me, seeming to deliberately shoot in circles around me and over my head, although no more bullets were aimed directly at me.

Despite my abilities and the way I could block bullets with air walls, I wasn't sure how to get out of this. It was the first time in a while they weren't trying to kill me, but I wasn't sure why.

I could feel Zephyr flying away, but he suddenly stopped.

Aella? he asked.

As he did, I tried to take control of the plants around me and grow them as a protective barrier, but none of them held for long under the fire, and the shooters targeted anything I threw up.

Beginning to lose control and drain myself, I slowly raised my hands.

Sorry, Zephyr. Looks like plans have changed. I can't get out of this circle.

I'm coming back to get you.

No! They'll tear your wings to shreds. Stay back. Find somewhere to hide or transform and then follow on.

But...

Zephyr. We have to get to Jacobs. We will get to Jacobs.

I projected confidence Zephyr's way, hoping he couldn't feel any other emotions leaking out of me along. In truth, I was terrified. These men could kill me.

As the pilot of the helicopter I'd landed got out and finally disentangled himself, I focused on him. As he walked over, he wore a kinder expression than I'd expected, and I got the feeling I'd earned a reprieve by saving his life.

"I want to speak to Jacobs," I said. "The guy in charge of all of this."

A moment later, someone pulled a black bag over my head, and my hands were grabbed and tied.

Had I been at full power I could easily have pushed them back, but I was exhausted from flying all night and having to defend us. I also suspected they'd just shoot me, and I was vulnerable.

Sen stayed tucked up in my pack. I could feel that she was now awake so I didn't draw any attention to her. With any luck she'd be ignored, but they quickly took my bow, arrows, and pack and emptied my pockets.

I felt a slight tug as Sen and my pack were moved away from me, but she projected an image and let me know that she was on the passenger seat of a car. With any luck, I'd be bundled into the back of the same car.

Trying not to panic but not enjoying being unable to see anything, I allowed myself to be manhandled into the back of another car, my awareness of Sen letting me know she was in the car behind us and heading in the same direction.

It helped me relax to also feel Zephyr. I wasn't sure where he was, but he was coming after us, and he didn't feel like he was very far away.

Can you tell where they're taking us? I asked Zephyr, wondering how he was traveling and if he was in human form or not right now.

They're taking you toward Jacobs for now. At least, it appears so.

I sighed. For now, that would have to do. It would only take one moment for me to put an end to this. I planned to do my best despite being captured.

While I sat in the back of the car, I felt for the air around and worked out the shapes of who I was with. I had a person on each side of me. At a guess, I'd have said they were soldiers, and they were both carrying guns that were trained on me.

I didn't like my chances of stopping bullets at close range, so I stayed still. No one spoke to me or each other, and we drove for what felt like an age.

Zephyr didn't follow closely, but he never got so far away I couldn't feel him, which I was extremely grateful for. Whatever happened, we'd still mostly be together.

CHAPTER NINETEEN

Eventually, the car came to a stop. Zephyr was still some way behind, but he was coming closer, so the strange feeling in my stomach was fading. I felt Sen move. She seemed panicked, but she soon settled down, swaying back and forth in the pack as someone carried it.

By the time they got me out of the car, Sen was sitting somewhere and cautiously looking out of the pack, and Zephyr was stationary a few hundred yards behind me.

Looks like another small compound, but this one is better guarded than the last. Zephyr's voice seemed loud in my head after talking to him while he was farther away, and it made me feel more comforted.

Can you get inside? I asked.

I think so. I'm back in human form and dressed in an agent's suit. Should be able to manage the rest based on Erlan's information.

I sighed. At least Zephyr was going to be getting into the building the way we'd originally planned, even if I was still a prisoner.

Allowing myself to be taken deeper into the compound, I tried to remember which route they were taking me, using Zephyr's position and the number of steps to get an idea of what direction and how far. It wasn't perfect, but it would have to do.

Not that I was sure if I'd remember the route, but I thought loudly, and I hoped Zephyr would hear and memorize some of it as well.

I was taken to a small room and locked inside. When the men walked away, I reached up and pulled the bag off my head. I was in a padded cell, similar to those I'd have expected to find in a psychiatric institute. The door in front of me was thick and made of metal. There was a small window with a shutter on it at about face height.

Walking closer, I inspected it. It didn't look as if it could be easily opened from this side but I reached out to the air around it with my mind. I was pretty sure I could blow it open as I had the bolts of the weapons locker in the last compound. I was also fairly sure that if I did, it wouldn't buckle or break, and I could put it back. If Sen could get to me, I might be able to sneak her inside.

That said, I was pretty sure there were going to be guards on the outside of the room.

"I want to talk to Jacobs," I said. "I know he's here. I've got something to tell him."

No one responded, so I repeated it a little louder. I was pretty sure I heard someone shift their feet on the other side of the door a moment later, but no one came to the door, pulled back the shutter, or responded.

Turning around, I checked out the rest of the room. I noticed a small camera in one corner and waved at it, wondering who would be watching. I then sat down on the middle of the floor and reached down into the earth and the building around me. I could feel the roots of trees nearby and the bedrock the building foundations had been built into.

I focused on making a tunnel out of the room, starting just under the floor and burrowing out toward Zephyr. It took a while, and I had to compress the earth, moving it slowly so it didn't cause any tremors. Of course, I had no idea if it was going to be needed, but I was good with having a contingency plan. I was also significantly less likely to be taxing my powers for a while.

When I was feeling worn out by the task, I stopped and got back to my feet. I was starving and getting bored.

I moved to the door again, aware Sen was also getting bored, stuck in the pack at the edge of a desk somewhere, the room full of agents. She'd scurried under the desk a couple of times, trying to work out how to get closer to me, but from where she was, she couldn't see the door, and I'd encouraged her to wait for now.

There was still time for her to find me. It didn't appear as though I was going to be taken to Jacobs in a hurry, and the thought of the food in my bag tempted me to get her to bring me some, but I had enough sense not to make the request. Instead, I urged Sen to wait in the bag and hope she wasn't caught.

Thankfully, no one asked me where the mythicals were as if they believed they'd caught me alone. It might have helped that I'd been seen a few times recently, alone or without both Sen and Zephyr, and not everyone had caught on to me having bonded with the myconid as well as the dragon.

Of course, Zephyr was also busy. He'd made his way around the whole building and checked it out from different angles, working out the best way to get in.

I think they're still looking for me, he said while I paced the room. *There's a lot of aircraft activity, and they've got soldiers coming and going.*

Can you get into the building?

I've heard enough chatter that I think I can. I'm going to need to ambush some men as they approach.

I felt scared for Zephyr, but I had to remind myself that he had all my abilities while he was in human form. And he looked like one of them. It shouldn't be too difficult for him to get an advantage.

Waiting for the mixture of the right moment and for an idea of where Jacobs was in the building wasn't my idea of fun, but I was closer to my goal than I'd ever been. At least I hoped so.

After a few more minutes of waiting, I felt Zephyr come closer to the compound again, moving faster than he could run as a human but slower than he could fly as a dragon.

I've taken an agent's car and badge. Should get me in okay.

I exhaled. That was one less problem to worry about. Most of the agents wore sunglasses, which would give him the option to cover his eyes. I imagined him swaggering up to the doors and into the building, swiping his card and striding along as if he owned the place.

The tension I'd barely realized had been mounting eased as he came closer and must have come inside, a thrill of delight washing from him to me via our bond.

Trying to appear normal from the outside, I went to the door and called for Jacobs again. This time I banged on it with my fists, and then I started to pace even more frantically.

It was time to start turning up the heat and make this work in our favor.

I acted agitated, calling out that something was wrong. Then I started to yell about bonds and being away from Zephyr for too long. Demanding to see Jacobs.

I stopped short of collapsing, but I began to make a distressing sort of keening noise the way a kitten might call for its mother. This finally had an effect. The men on the other side pulled open the shutter. At first, I didn't stop, but then I calmed myself, got myself back to my feet, and stumbled over to the door.

"I can't be away from my dragon much longer. It's going to kill me. I have to see Jacobs."

"We're not taking you anywhere. You can die in there for all we care."

I burst out laughing, sounding manic.

"Doesn't matter if I die; it won't stop them from coming. Thousands of them. Zephyr was just the first."

This got their attention, although they pretended it hadn't and slammed the shutter closed again. Instead of ignoring it, however, one of the guards outside stomped down the hallway. I sank down, keeping my face away from the cameras as I grinned. It appeared my little performance had done the job.

Now for Zephyr and Sen to do their parts.

I reached out to see what Sen was doing. Her mind was full of images I could use to my advantage. She'd gotten under the desk again, carrying what she needed from the pack and keeping it from the agent nearby.

As she glanced back, I saw that the guy was finally looking through my bag for whatever he thought might be of interest. I saw him pocket some of the cash, and it made me grateful it wasn't all in one place.

One of the few things my mother had taught me that had come in handy since I'd discovered I was an elf was that thieves tended to find one stash and stop looking. She'd told me to split up large amounts of cash and hide them in different places in different bags, some better hidden than others.

That way, no matter what happened, you always had some left, and you were never stuck. It was supposed to have been a vacation tip, but it had just saved the organization an awful lot of money, or me, depending on whether they asked for it back after this was all over.

I eased myself into a more comfortable position as if the worst of the pain had passed and then sat upright, rocking back and forth as I stared into the distance and followed Zephyr and Sen with my mind.

Sen waited until Zephyr appeared, drawing all eyes to him. He went over to the nearest agent and asked where he might find Jacobs' office, professing to have some very important information from LA.

The agents looked at him strangely at first.

"Come on. Out with it. I have to give him this information on the current state of the untagged mythicals in California. It's crucial that we deal with the situation swiftly before it gets out of hand. I've got eggs, man. Lots of eggs."

Sen used the distraction of Zephyr's monologue to

make a dash for the next desk, and then the next until she was in the corridor and rushing down it, bouncing along until she found the air ducts and some vents. She threw herself up the wall, climbing it with one hand and her feet like someone might abseil but moving in the opposite direction.

It made me a little motion-sick, but she was soon holding onto the grill. She let out a little shiver at the cold air pumping out but got to work pulling out the screws.

Down the hallway, I could just about hear Zephyr talking about a cave full of eggs as if he didn't realize he wasn't talking to Jacobs and everyone might want to know.

Of course, it was complete crap, but it was going to add to my story, and it was going to get Jacobs' attention. And that was all we needed.

Sen was soon finding her way through the air vents. I pulled back from her projected images a little to continue my act.

"Come on, you're killing me in here without Zephyr. I have to see Jacobs and get back to my dragon."

It smacked of arrogance and I was laughed at again, but it wasn't a confident laugh, and it came from a different agent. As Sen found what she was looking for, a larger vent, and Zephyr was directed up a couple of floors and to the back of the building. The guard finally came back to join his buddy in front of my cell.

The shutter flicked open, and I was glared at. I crouched, my arms clutched over my stomach, but I tried to straighten as if it were important I soldier through what I was feeling.

"Looks like the boss wants to hear what you've got to

say before we let whatever this is finish you off," the guard said. "We'd better not keep him waiting."

Again, I had to hide a smile, this time turning it into a grimace. I thanked my lucky stars that the guards weren't adept at reading body language as I shuffled along between them, being escorted closer and closer to both my mythicals while everyone else was none the wiser.

I'm there, Zephyr said a moment later. *They asked me to wait to see him in a small room outside.*

Sen there, the tiny wood dryad added a moment later.

I was on my way, and that meant we were finally going to get this whole thing over and done with.

Walking up the stairs wasn't easy while pretending to be in agony, but one of the guards grabbed my arm and acted as if he were dragging me when in fact, he was helping me with more gentleness than I'd expected. I made a mental note that he was a soft touch as we turned into the next hallway.

I spotted the room Zephyr was in but gave it no more of my attention than I ought to. Instead, I hurried toward what was obviously Jacobs' office.

The guards knocked, and a familiar male voice commanded us to go inside.

"The great Aella-Faye, elven princess, or some such nonsense, and dragon-tamer extraordinaire," he said as he came over to me.

I exhaled and sank to my knees as if I still hurt.

"I didn't tame him," I said when no one else spoke. "The rest is about right, though."

This made him chuckle, and I watched him wave the guards out of the room.

Jacobs walked closer, but he stopped far enough away that even if I lunged, I wouldn't be able to reach him.

"Jacobs," I added. "I guess we're meeting at last."

"My men informed me that you had something to say," he said as he crouched so he could see my face better.

I made a pantomime of fighting back pain and trying to breathe, and then I met his gaze.

"Yes. I have a lot to say," I replied.

CHAPTER TWENTY

For a moment, Jacobs and I studied each other while Zephyr and Sen finished dealing with the guards outside. Sen dropped a gas bomb on both the guards outside and Jacobs' receptionist, and Zephyr caught them before either could fall to the floor, then locked them in a room.

I saw all this through my link with Sen. Before Jacobs could do anything else, I stood.

"Ah, not in as much pain as you appeared," he said, backing up.

He made it look as if he was going back to his desk to sit, but I was pretty sure he was scared. He reached toward the desk, but I blasted his chair away from it before he could touch anything. Despite the allies I had just outside the door, I didn't want him to call any more agents.

"I think you better sit where you are." I moved closer, wanting to make sure the distance between us wasn't too far.

"Have you come to try to kill me, then?" Jacobs asked, acting as if I hadn't just blasted him back several feet. "Do you think you can finish this by cutting the head off the beast?"

"No. I rather imagine this agency is like the Hydra. I cut your head off, and three will grow back," I replied as I moved closer. "But even if that weren't the case, I have no intention of killing anyone. I think you're all misguided fools. But we've got a lot to discuss, you and I."

"I don't think so, although I'm sure you might." Jacobs went to get back up again, but I blasted him with air again, and I used the plant on the shelf behind him to pin him to the chair.

"After all the things I've been able to do, do you really think you have much choice but to chat to me now? Just because I won't kill you, it doesn't mean I won't make you sit there until you've answered my questions, Jacobs."

"You can't force me to."

"Maybe not. But I'm going to ask anyway, and I guess we'll have to see what you have to say for yourself. Maybe we can both walk out of this room happy with this meeting."

Jacobs looked like he was going to fight the restraints and me for a moment, but eventually, he looked at me and relaxed.

"If you think you have the upper hand here, you don't. It's not going to be long before either the distance in that bond of yours breaks you or my men get here and I have them shoot you."

"Then humor me," I replied and sat down, still making it look as if I was exhausted. "I want to know if it's you behind all this? All the hate, all the twisting of the media. Is it you giving the orders?"

"It might as well be. I have oversight, of course, but they don't care what I tell them," he replied more honestly than I'd have expected.

"Did I really kill anyone?"

"I thought you'd ask that. Do you really expect me to admit the truth?"

"If you're going to finish me and my kind off, the least you could do is let me know if I took anyone with me. I'd ask you to let me die with a clear conscience, but I don't think you care about that. I'd still like to know how powerful I truly am."

Jacobs looked thoughtful for a moment but eventually nodded.

"You killed a few men at that battle on the road and another at the compound you were at before. Or someone did. I know there are other powerful elves, and you sometimes team up. I've seen the footage."

I exhaled. Crawley had killed the man at the compound and at least one at the large battle.

"And the second attack on the compound. The men in the guard tower that caught fire."

"Both lived. They had significant injuries. They'll have scars, as will others, but we've killed far more of your kind than you've ever killed of ours."

"You see it as us and you, then?" I snapped, losing my temper. I felt a rush of calm from Zephyr.

"It always has been. You're scum. The world belongs to humans now. Elves, dragons, and all the other pathetic races you call mythicals have had their time. It's long gone, nothing but a myth and a memory."

I fought the urge to tell him he was wrong, letting Jacobs talk now that he'd gotten going.

"I'm going to see every single one of your kind wiped from the face of this planet, and I'm going to enjoy doing it. Humanity will call me a hero for it."

"You've been making sure of that, haven't you?" I prompted as he paused. "Anything else you've done to convince them other than lying about how many people I've killed?"

"Oh, so many things. Too many to mention. You don't have time." He laughed, and I had to decide whether to glare at him or look pained. It only made him laugh harder.

He inched a hand closer, and it made the smirk on his face grow.

"Why?" I asked a moment later, pretty sure we didn't have much longer. "What made you hate my kind so much that you'd go to these lengths to see us destroyed?"

There was silence when I finished speaking, and I started to suspect I wasn't going to get an answer. Jacobs was serious now, staring at me, his face revealing every ounce of hatred he held for me. I'd wondered why so many times. Would he answer?

"Your kind are born arrogant. If I don't stop you, you'll make us all slaves to the way of life you think is best. You'll breed and take over every institution, every school, and every government until humanity becomes nothing but a lower class, unable to perform magic and there for you to subjugate."

"That's a pretty big claim without proof," I shot back, sure there was something that must have caused it—something bad to have given him such a warped opinion.

"Without proof?" Indignation made him spit, and he tore up and out of the chair, the anger that came with it giving him strength.

Still kneeling on his floor, I winced in pain and clutched my stomach. He needed to think he had time to continue. That he had me right where he wanted me just a little longer.

"I have all the proof I need. Almost thirty years ago, a young boy wandered somewhere he shouldn't. Found some kids playing a game, somehow keeping a ball in the air. Made it look like some parlor trick," he said as he walked over and crouched in front of me. "That little boy asked if he could play. The kids said yes, but when they realized he was human and he didn't have magic like they did, they bullied him. Used their magic to tease him, wreck his clothes."

"They were just kids," I said through gritted teeth.

"Maybe, but then their parents noticed us. Did they help me or punish their offspring for such behavior? No, they used their own magic on me. Blasted me out of the field, and the kids ran off back the way they'd come with their floating ball."

I opened my mouth to speak, but Jacobs grabbed my chin and moved his face to an inch away from mine.

"I told my pa, and he got his brother and the neighbor and his dog, and they went back with me the next day. They weren't there, but their little caravan was. We trashed it. Told them they weren't welcome. Do you know what they did after that?"

I tried to shake my head, but I felt for them. Their kids had been wrong to bully him if they'd truly done what he described, but the parents had probably been terrified of what Jacobs and his family had done.

"What do you think they did?" he asked as he shook me.

"I don't know," I replied, genuinely wincing this time.

"They used their powers to rebuild it, and then they drove right past me the next morning, their wagon perfectly sparkling new again. The little elves even had the cheek to wave at me and throw their ball my way one last time. I still have it. A reminder that your kind can't be trusted and are nothing but—"

"Had it ever occurred to you that they might have given you their ball to say sorry?" I asked. "If they loved playing with it and they threw it to you, they probably hoped you'd see it as a peace offering."

As I spoke, I got to my feet, using my powers to push back and overpower him.

Jacobs laughed despite struggling against me. It was clear he didn't believe my response.

"All of my encounters with other mythicals have shown me time and time again that they just want to hide; they just want to get along. And your story only confirms that," I continued as I drove him back, blasting air at him until he was sitting in his chair again.

"You're wrong. They were arrogant—"

"If those elves had wanted to retaliate, they didn't need to throw a ball at you. They rebuilt their home in only a night and made it look as good as new. They could have killed you for what you did to their home. Had every right to press charges, if nothing else. Instead, they fled. Those are not the actions of arrogant mythicals."

Jacobs tried to speak again, but I'd heard enough. I

wrapped the leaves of a plant around his mouth to muffle his words and got to my feet. Dropping all the pretense of being in any kind of difficulty, I walked toward him.

"I could kill you now," I said as I sat down on the edge of his desk. "You've done nothing but hunt me because I exist since the moment I found Zephyr. I've been targeted by a sniper because of you. I've had to sleep rough in caves and while Zephyr kept me safe in the sky because of you. I've had good friends die defending themselves because of you. I'm pretty sure that's bullying. By your logic, that gives me every right to trash your home and murder you."

I paused, watching a bead of sweat run down his forehead. He was terrified.

"But I'm not going to do that since your logic is flawed. You escalated your behavior back when you were young. There was no way that those kids deserved to have their home wrecked. And you've been escalating your attacks on mythicals ever since. It ends now."

"There's nothing you can do to stop me," Jacobs said as he managed to break through the leaves. "The people hate you. I've made them hate you and your kind just as you deserve."

I rolled my eyes and walked toward the door.

"We're done here," I said as I reached for the door handle.

"No, we're not. You're not walking out of here alive. Men!" Jacobs struggled out of the chair again, but there were no men for him to call, and I simply walked out of the office and shut the door behind me.

To make sure I had an easy route out while Sen and

Zephyr came to me, I grabbed a chair and propped it under the door's handle.

By the time I was done, Zephyr and Sen were standing beside me, Sen holding the recorder Zephyr had brought in with his briefcase.

Got it all? I asked.

Sen record. She pressed play, playing me a crackly recording of Jacobs telling his story.

I grinned as she stopped it again, then Zephyr tucked the small device into a pocket.

Right. Time to go get the rest of my things and then get out of here, I projected. Sen jumped over to my shoulder, and Zephyr hung back. He was going to bring up the rear, and if things went south, he'd get out of a window and switch back to his dragon form.

Reaching for the air, I whipped it into a spinning vortex. The process was far easier in the confined space. With it swirling and picking up dust and debris, I added anything I could find that would make people back up, including staples from the receptionist's desk.

We hurried through the building, heading down and then toward the agency offices. Along the way, Zephyr and Sen gave me instructions and let me know who might be up ahead and if they were likely to shoot.

Zephyr moved to shield me when an agent noticed us near the bottom of the stairs. A bullet pinged off his chest and the veiled scales before he threw up an air wall to defend us both.

I hit the agent with the tornado and wrenched the gun out of his hands. As the agent plastered himself to the wall to get out of the way and brought an arm up to shield himself, Zephyr shot him with a dart gun, and he went down.

The noise drew more agents, but most of the shots they fired were forced off target by my miniature tornado, and the rest were stopped by the air wall or Zephyr.

It was an effective combination, and it made me grateful that I had Zephyr along with me. I couldn't have wielded this much magic alone, even if someday I might be able to. With more practice at making tornadoes, I might one day, but not today.

The agents didn't give up. More of them came, and this group was so determined that some of them tried to walk through the twister to get to me.

I focused on swirling it even faster, the debris cutting at the skin of the first agent who somehow made it through. Zephyr hit him with a trank, and he went down.

Fighting to keep focused and in control of the spinning air, I pushed on until the twister was right by the door to the main office. There were agents in both directions, some having come inside when they heard shooting.

Take the twister down the corridor, Zephyr said, shooting another agent. *I'll get the pack.*

I considered arguing, but Zephyr sounded confident. I decided to trust him, so I pushed the twister farther on as he made for the door. A moment later, I heard more bullets hit his scales and bounce off, lodging in all sorts of other places.

"You traitor," an agent yelled at him, making me grin. They didn't realize he was Zephyr, and that was fine by me.

Although I was now vulnerable, I still had the advantage, and I continued to press forward and try not to worry about the battle I couldn't see that was being waged to my right.

Another agent came through the twister, his skin cut in a hundred places. I blasted him with air to push him back, Zephyr still somewhere behind me with my gun.

A minute later, the agent's office went quiet.

Zephyr, you okay? I asked, focusing on the agents I still had to deal with. Although I couldn't feel any pain from him, I couldn't help but worry.

Yup, just getting the pack. I like the outfit you have in here. Don't want to lose it.

All our money is in there too, I replied, grinning.

We definitely need that. It pays for pizza.

Letting out a laugh, I barreled the twister into yet another agent and felt Zephyr come back out of the office behind me. He strode to my side and then moved in front again, my pack on his shoulder.

A few more shots from the dart gun he carried, and the compound was silent. I let the twister dissipate before moving on.

There will be at least a few more men outside. There were soldiers on the gate.

Let's take a side route out, then.

Better idea, he replied, reaching down to the nearest agent and grabbing the zip ties in his pocket. I raised my eyebrows as he snapped them over my wrists and Sen jumped into my pack.

Use a black bag, too, I said. *It will look more authentic.*

For a moment Zephyr hesitated, but then he walked back to the office, and one floated toward us on the wind he controlled. I snatched it out of the air and pulled it on over my head before letting my hands drop.

I felt Zephyr's strong grip on my arm a moment later, and then he was walking me out and back toward the car he'd stolen.

Several voices called to each other, but I couldn't hear what they said.

"Boss wants her moved somewhere even more secure. The dragon has come closer, and she's perked up a bit. Made a mess in there and tranked some of our guys. You'd best send in another couple of men to help secure up the place," Zephyr replied. "Jacobs is pissed."

No one argued, and I was shoved into the back of the car. Sen and the pack went with Zephyr in the front.

Zephyr started up the engine and drove out, only pausing at the gates.

As we drove out of the compound, I couldn't help but laugh. We'd done it, and Jacobs really was going to be pissed.

CHAPTER TWENTY-ONE

As Zephyr finished becoming a dragon again, I felt a pang of regret that it was necessary, but we had farther to go, and we needed to ditch the car we'd stolen.

We'd driven a good few miles before the radio had burst to life and let us know our game was up and that I shouldn't have left the compound. As Zephyr found somewhere good to pull over and hide the car, we listened to their confusion over who the human male with me had been. It made me chuckle.

After everything Jacobs had put me through and all the ways he'd made me look bad, it felt amazing to return the favor.

However, we needed to get in the air and get going again.

I'd briefly used the communication stone. Erlan and Ronan were together and on their way. We needed to backtrack to meet up with them, but they needed the recording we had so it could be backed up. Then we could make use of it.

Thankfully, the events at the compound had taken up most of the day, and we'd be flying late at night again. The sky was darkening as we got into the air.

Although we still needed to be careful, I cared less now whether we were seen. It was only important that we weren't seen with Erlan and Ronan before they'd gotten a backup of the conversation and taken it to the Sanctuary.

Chris and Minsheng were also moving about the country. They would be our next stop, but I didn't know where and would have to rely on Ronan to make sure we all found each other in the end.

A moment later, Zephyr gave me a nod, and Sen settled into my jacket again.

Let's go get the rest of our stuff, he said, his scaly mouth opening in the best grin the dragon could form. I wasn't going to argue, but part of me was worried it wouldn't be where we'd left it, or we wouldn't find the lake and the boathouse I'd stuffed the strange material that hid us from heat-sensitive scanners in.

And we needed to fly all the way there.

Finally propelling myself into the air as Zephyr joined me, I got a good look at the damage to his wings. Once again, spending time as a human had given them a rest, and I was sure the holes were smaller.

However it worked to heal him, I was more than grateful it did. I'd been worried that he was never going to be able to fly properly again.

We came together in the air and I settled into position on his back, comfortable and thankful that we were familiar with each other and this felt so natural. I'd been tense the entire time we'd been apart and I'd been a prisoner, even if I hadn't put up as much of a fight as I could have.

The strategy the helicopters had used had been effective, and I knew I'd come close to dying yet again, but for some reason, they hadn't killed me. It bothered me that Jacobs seemed to want nothing but my death. Admittedly, it appeared that not all his agents wanted me dead. However, I wondered what would happen if I was ever in that situation again.

I didn't think I would get mercy a second time.

There won't be a second time, Zephyr's voice cut through my thoughts, letting me know he was hearing my fears. *We're going to stop this agency once and for all. We're almost there.*

I sighed and focused. He was right. We just needed to keep going a little longer.

Trying not to think about it, I focused on helping Zephyr fly and listening out for anything else in the sky with us. No doubt Jacobs would already be looking for us again, and I didn't think it would take them long to find the car we'd abandoned. They wouldn't be stupid enough to think we weren't in the air again.

Flight was our sole advantage in being able to move through enemy territory and cover large distances quickly.

As the night grew even darker, it started raining, and I had to use my abilities to keep the majority of the water off Sen and me to keep us from getting drenched. If I wanted to preserve my powers, there wasn't much I could do about Zephyr, but he assured me it wasn't a problem.

Guilt gnawed at me as the scales around me grew more and more shiny and slippery but the small patch I occupied remained dry, the air flowing around me and taking the water with it.

After another hour or so, Zephyr started circling lower until I could see the outline of the boat house and the lake where we'd stowed our stuff. We landed beside it, and I slid off Zephyr's back into the sticky mud beside the building. I frowned as I noticed the door we'd gone through wasn't as I'd left it and there were footprints around it.

Looks like the agents might have been here. Want me in human form again? Zephyr asked.

No. I'll go in. I can be careful, and we need to save your energy. I'm going to need you as a dragon.

I heard Zephyr sigh, and he brought his head near the opening anyway.

If you see an agent, I'll fill it with gas. You can take a bubble of clean air in with you if you need.

Although I wasn't one hundred percent convinced about the idea as a method of defense in this situation, I didn't argue and went inside. Zephyr wanted to protect me, and I would let him do what he could when logic didn't dictate otherwise.

The interior was shrouded in darkness, and I had to use a flashlight to see the boats well enough to navigate to the one I'd stowed our stuff on. Just inside the building, I paused for a moment, looking for signs of movement or that someone might still be there.

All I saw was the boat shed, more footprints, and a few messy areas that the agents had searched.

I went over to the large boat and looked inside. I'd shut it back up, but it was not exactly how I'd left it. There were muddy footprints going into the living room. I was pretty sure I hadn't been the one to leave them.

Reaching for the air inside, I tried to detect if there was another living person, but I couldn't sense any movements or breathing. Still wary, I walked into the main area of the boat and looked around. Some of the cupboards had been rifled through, but I noticed that the one I'd stuffed our second pack in was still completely untouched.

I walked over to it and opened it. Moving the ropes aside, I found everything we'd hidden. Although I wasn't sure exactly how it had escaped notice, I was grateful. There were other compartments that also hadn't been touched, so I was pretty sure I could put it down to luck and a sloppy agent who didn't believe we'd hidden anything there.

Whatever the truth was, I didn't have time to find out. I hurried back out to Zephyr and we put on the jackets, then I slung the pack around his neck and tucked the rest into my pack.

We got back into the air again. The rain eased as we headed southwest.

We're not far from where Erlan and Ronan said they'd meet us, Zephyr said a moment later, and I almost kicked myself for not getting out the communication stone and double-checking.

In the end, there was nothing we could do but fly on. I wasn't going to land somewhere we were vulnerable, and we still had a lot of ground to cover before the night was over.

Another hour ticked by, and my powers began to wane. I'd not eaten much and I'd been awake for a long time, barely getting any sleep anywhere. Zephyr had been awake even longer.

Almost ready to sleep, Zephyr said as I pulled the last energy drink from the bag and chugged it down. *Just need to find Erlan and Ronan.*

Zephyr came down a little lower so we could see the roads and fields better. I recognized the area we were in from the satellite imagery we'd studied. Once again, I marveled how my dragon always seemed to know exactly where he was and where he needed to be.

We flew on a little farther until we saw a large vehicle coming down the road. It looked like a celebrity tour bus or a massive show trailer, and it took up a lot of space.

Is that them? I asked Zephyr, but we had no way to tell without revealing ourselves.

Want me to fly down in front of them?

No, even if it is them, you could make them crash or give them a heart attack.

Zephyr rose again, and for a moment, we followed the bus as whoever was driving continued up the road. At the next turnout, they pulled over and we flew circles around them, trying to figure out if they were stopping for us or not.

When I saw the familiar shape of a centaur coming out of the side door, I exhaled with relief. Even if it wasn't Ronan, it was a mythical, and that meant it was an ally.

We swooped down and landed in the field beside it, and I slid off Zephyr's back.

A moment later, I made out Ronan, and we hurried to the vehicle.

"Get in," Ronan said. "We think we've had a tail for a while, but we're not sure. Best you're not seen."

I didn't intend to argue since Erlan also appeared, and between them, they opened a massive side hatch. Zephyr could just about squeeze inside. He settled into the middle of the vehicle. It had been hollowed out at the back to make room for him, and there was a living area for the humanoid mythicals at the front, including beds, a toilet, a shower, and a small kitchen.

"Where did you get this?" I asked. Ronan and Erlan both stood beside me, and we got on the road again with someone else driving.

"Organization dropped it off near the cabin, and Minsheng had Daisy drive us. He, Chris, and Iris are working on the rest of the plan."

"Iris?" I asked.

"She told us you'd trust her now. She didn't explain more than that," Ronan added.

I nodded at him. "Trust is a strong word, but this would be the third time she's come through for me when I've really needed it, and that is not something to ignore. She's an ally worth having."

"My assessment would be similar." The centaur bowed and then noticed Erlan standing beside him with a laptop in his hand. There was a gleam in the elf's eyes, and he was staring at me as if he was going to burst.

I reached into my pocket and pulled the recorder out before handing it over.

"You got it?" he asked, his eyes wide as he rushed to the nearest table.

When Sen hopped out of the pack to go join Zephyr, I

considered doing the same and leaving Erlan and Ronan to do what they needed to, but I was also starving, and I'd taxed my powers a lot.

Do you want food before sleep? I asked Zephyr, but he didn't reply, already dozing.

Zeph sleep, Sen replied for him, making me grin. As Ronan clopped to the front, going down a few steps toward the driver, I put my finger to my lips to let Erlan know to be quiet and mimed someone lying their head down on a pillow.

I walked to the small fridge. Erlan sat down and got to work with the transcript and backup audio while I made myself some sandwiches and grabbed a few other things that looked good from the array of food they'd stocked the bus with. I considered a soda, but I was pretty sure the sugar and caffeine would make it harder to sleep.

I sat down beside Erlan and helped him get everything we needed together while I stuffed my face.

With that done and a thumb drive nestled in a small pocket on the inside of my jacket, I went back to Zephyr and settled down beside him to sleep. Sen had fallen asleep as well, her small frame resting against one of Zephyr's ears. The moment I lay down beside Zephyr, his tail swished around and tucked me in close to his side.

Although we'd need to fly again at some point, I was hidden from Jacobs for now, and we could sleep while our friends took us to our final destination.

CHAPTER TWENTY-TWO

I yawned and stirred, feeling Zephyr shift beside me. Although I had no idea what time of day or night it was, I felt a lot better and was instantly aware that the engine was no longer rumbling.

We've stopped for gas and to pick up the rest of the crew, Zephyr said.

But the backup data was supposed to go to the Sanctuary, I replied, sitting up as fear gripped me.

Erlan and Ronan are already on the way back with it. The council has promised to protect it. Ronan only had to listen to it once. He said something about a detour. I think Jacobs' story had an impact.

I guess he didn't say why?

No, he said to keep your stone where you could access it and for me to resist it if it called to you.

I frowned. There was a chance that could be more than a little dangerous. Especially if we were in the middle of the last part of our plan to stop this whole thing once and for all.

Zephyr didn't appear concerned, and I needed to eat again, so I made my way back to the kitchen area and looked around for whoever our driver was.

The front seats were empty and there was no sign of anyone else, so I made my way back and got started on breakfast for everyone. Sen was happy to sit in some watered soil on the counter as I did so, but Zephyr was clearly hungry. An adorable purr came out of him as I cooked the sausages and bacon I took out of the fridge.

I was just plating up a massive breakfast for him when I heard the sound of people getting onto the bus.

Slightly wary, I didn't move or call out but reached for the air around me, preparing to defend us if needed.

I heard Chris laugh at something and I relaxed. Making my way toward the front again, I found Minsheng coming my way, carrying some bits of tech, a couple of his books, and a rolled blueprint.

"You look like crap," he said.

"Nice to see you too," I replied, although I grinned. He dropped everything he was carrying on the table and hugged me.

"Are you all in one piece?" he asked, concern written on his features.

It was only then that I noticed the massive bags under his eyes. He'd been worried or sleepless for one reason or another.

"We're just fine. Had a couple of hairy moments, but Zephyr was amazing, and Jacobs has bought every bit of our trick so far. What about you? You look stressed."

"Worried," he replied, running a hand through his hair. "I hope this works."

"Me too. But it should. If not, I'm now farther back than I was before we started this whole thing."

Minsheng didn't look like that was much of a comfort, but I didn't want to think about it anymore. This had to work. I wasn't going back to being hunted.

While everyone got ready to head out again, I had Chris show me the rest of the tech I was going to need to use and found out it was Daisy driving us.

We were all traveling together for a little longer, but as soon as it was night again, Zephyr, Sen, and I would get into the sky again.

It felt strange to be doing this alone again, but there was no one who could help us directly with this next part, and it was important I didn't drag anyone else into trouble.

"You'll get to safety as soon as you can?" I asked Minsheng. "I need you to keep them all out of it once it's all set up."

"It won't stop them charging us with crimes if this all goes wrong, but we've worked out how to get everyone into the lightest category possible," he replied.

I felt like he was keeping something from me. His response was vaguer than I'd hoped for, but I knew I couldn't stop them from doing what they felt was important. And in truth, I was grateful. I felt alone enough as it was.

With the sun setting, Zephyr, Sen, and I got ready. I donned the clothes I wanted to wear, a jacket fitting over the body armor made from Zephyr's scales. It made me look a little bulkier, but we'd made a few adjustments to it, and it fit me better than before. I looked as if I were wearing armor made for me now.

Zephyr was still in dragon form, and he was ready to get out of the space. It was really too small for him. It might have been wider than any other vehicle possible, but the bus was still a little too small for a full-grown dragon.

Sen settled into my jacket as she always did, and I put together the pack and equipment we would need for the next few hours. I only put in a few snacks and a single bottle of water. This was either going to work and I wouldn't need any of it, or it would go so badly I'd need far more than I could carry and I'd have to come back to the tour bus.

After giving everyone a quick hug and checking the coast was clear outside, I opened the large hatch for Zephyr to get out and followed him. Minsheng gave me a nod and then closed it behind us.

We didn't talk as we got into the air and flew to our final destination. There was nothing to say. At least, not yet. We knew what we had to do.

Minsheng had given us a rundown with the blueprints. We knew where we were going and what our main target would be, even if we didn't know what forces we'd be facing.

Our mission was going to be about speed more than anything else.

Trying not to worry, we flew together, me riding on Zephyr's back at his normal speed, only making an air barrier around Sen and me to control the flow of air and reduce the resistance.

I needed as much of my power as I could save for what we were about to do.

We flew for a couple of hours, the tour bus following along behind at a slower speed, having to follow roads and get there in a different way.

Of course, they didn't need to get the whole way there. They just needed to be close enough to pick up my signal.

Finally, our target lay before us, a lit beacon on the ground that was impossible to miss.

The White House.

It was time to have a chat with the man who ran the country.

We circled a couple of times for Zephyr to get a good look at what we were up against.

All our information made it clear that as soon as there was an attack or a possible threat that the President was whisked down to a bunker somewhere in the White House.

I didn't want to have to fight my way all the way down to it. That meant we needed to get to the President before anyone had time to decide a threat was coming.

There's not much movement. It's as quiet as Chris said it would be.

Remind me to thank whoever got him the information, I replied, butterflies turning my stomach into a mess, my pulse beginning to race. Were we really about to attack the White House?

Ready? Zephyr asked me.

No, but we can't back out now, and I'm not going to get any more ready.

I focused on the target and took control of the air and ground as Zephyr dropped us toward the lawn.

While he did, I turned the small camera on my jacket on

and checked the transmission light. It wasn't going to be high quality, but it was going to be enough.

When we were still a hundred feet or so up, people spotted us and shouted. I quickly blasted them off their feet, and Zephyr exhaled before anyone could get a gas mask on.

Several of the Secret Service agents guarding the building went down, knocked out.

As Zephyr landed, I powered off his back and Sen jumped forward, rolling, running, and jumping toward one of the downed men.

I pulled out the dart gun I had and shot another pair of Secret Service men as they came running around the side of the building. I stepped up to the window outside the Oval Office and took control of all the plants in the room while I planted seeds by the window.

Pinning the President in place, I set the air in the room swirling and blasted back Secret Service agents as they came running toward him in an attempt to free him from the natural prison.

I could feel and hear their panic, but I needed to separate the man before anyone could get him away from me. Growing runners from the seeds I'd planted up the building, I fought the President's guards as they tried to get to him.

Shots rang out to my right. Zephyr was at the main entrance and stopping people from getting to us. He exhaled into the door as someone came out, his mind projecting the image to me briefly.

Sen then did the same, warning me as more soldiers came hurtling toward us from the right. A bullet hit the armor I wore and made a hole in my jacket before I could fire darts in their direction.

Guiding them with my mind, I knocked them all out and went back to the President. The glass was bulletproof, but the walls were made of something I could control.

I crumbled one wall just enough to allow the runners through, and it bound the President to his chair before he could break out of the grip of the weaker plants that were already inside the room.

The Secret Service agents and the President panicked even worse, and I felt sorry for the man. He probably thought he was about to die.

Although I needed to keep him there, I also needed to get inside the building so I could talk to him. But we'd already accounted for this problem. Sen came running over, bounding up the beanstalks and other plants now growing up the walls and up to the window.

With her feeding me a picture of the room so I could keep an eye on what I was controlling, I made my way back to Zephyr. I found him facing off against several agents wearing gas masks.

One was pinned under Zephyr's large claws, but he couldn't get the gas mask off to knock the man out. I hit him with a dart instead. The agent went limp, and Zephyr pounced on another as she tried to turn her aim on me. I shot her as well, then I hurried to the main door, pushing an air blast before me.

As soon as I was inside, I pulled on a gas mask and checked the image Sen was projecting. The Secret Service agents in the Oval Office were back on their feet and trying to get the President free. A moment later, I had them wrapped up in vines and pinned to the desk as well.

With them distracted again, I refocused on getting inside.

Zephyr had pulled the door off its hinges and exhaled a thick gas into the corridor beyond. Not wanting to have my vision obscured, I took control of the air before I stepped in. It acted like a small bubble that was carried with me. I reached to feel through the gas for more Secret Service agents.

There was someone up ahead, but they were cowering behind something. Maybe a desk. I hurried over to the position, my dart gun held out in front of me and my air bubble and gas mask keeping me safe for now.

I found a receptionist or female staffer crouched under the edge of the desk.

"Are you going to cause any trouble?" I asked her as I moved closer.

She shook her head and shivered as I grabbed her arm. I almost helped her up before I remembered she wouldn't be able to breathe. The desk had a pocket of air under it, and she'd been safe, not breathing in the gas.

Not sure what else to do, I cleared some gas out of her way.

"Go on, go," I said when she hesitated.

Without another glance, she ran out, and I watched her head past Zephyr.

I checked in with Sen and found the five men in the Oval Office tied up. Although I'd seen the blueprints of the building and I knew roughly how to get to where I wanted to go, I still needed to be careful. I couldn't afford to make any mistakes or let my guard down.

Making sure my bubble was secure, I walked deeper into the building, leaving Zephyr and Sen behind to guard the rear.

CHAPTER TWENTY-THREE

I didn't meet any resistance at first. The gas Zephyr had breathed into the building started to thin, but if anyone else lurked in the building intent on attacking me, I couldn't feel them with the air or see them. We'd already taken out a good twenty to thirty servicemen and staffers between us, so it was possible there wasn't anyone else there.

I spotted a door slightly ajar, the corner of a cellphone visible as someone poked it out just far enough to use the camera.

Slightly worried it would aid someone trying to shoot me, I threw up more air and slowly moved closer, but the wielder merely followed me with it. I used my abilities to push the door open without getting close.

The room contained three staffers, all of them terrified.

"I won't hurt you. I just needed to know you weren't going to try to shoot me," I said. "If you want to move somewhere else, now is a good time. Otherwise, I'm going to shut this door and lock it."

None of them responded. Not even the woman filming had anything to say to me.

I pulled the door shut again and grabbed a nearby chair to shove under the handle. With that done, I checked in on Sen. Two of the Secret Service agents had helped each other get free and had returned to the President to try to get him out of his chair.

Although I was still in control of the plants, I could feel that they didn't have the water or the nutrients for me to grow them much farther. I needed to get into the Oval Office and I needed to get in there now.

Trying not to be so rushed that I didn't check for enemies, I jogged down the next corridor with a tight wall of air around me and my dart gun out. Although I wished I had Zephyr with me, there was no way he could come inside.

As the gas dissipated, I took off the gas mask and formed a tornado, glad I'd had a bit more practice at the formidable attack. The second I had something semi-decent formed, I pushed it down the hallway ahead of me and jogged on.

It wasn't easy to do so many things at once and remember where I was going, but I was confident I was going in the right direction when I saw two more Secret Service agents outside a door. They had their guns ready, and one was talking into his mic when I came around the corner.

I blasted their weapons with air, knocking one of them loose and sending bullets flying. The tornado took care of their next attempts to stop me, although the weaponless guard tried to run at me through it.

As soon as he was on my side of the tornado, I shot him with the dart gun and knocked him out. Taking a moment to aim, I shot the second. I ran to the door and grabbed the handle to pull it open, but it didn't budge.

There was no keyhole and nothing that indicated a locking mechanism. Another glance at Sen's view showed the Secret Service agents pulling the President out of the chair. I didn't have time to try to pick a lock. I needed to get into the room.

Backing to a safe distance, I drew my bow and dropped my dart gun.

Then I grabbed one of my explosive arrows, took aim at the door near the handle, and fired.

There was a loud bang and a flash of fire when my arrow found its target. Had I not formed a barrier of air around myself, I was pretty sure I'd have been sent flying and possibly been deafened as well. I was still pushed back by the shockwave.

I ran through the opening and looked for the President myself now that I was inside the Oval Office without having to look through Sen.

The President was between four Secret Service agents, hunkered down on the far side of the room, and they were heading around the desk to go through another of the doors out on the opposite side.

Before they could open it, I blasted air to pin them all in place and hurried into the room.

Two of the guards turned and shot at me. Already bored with people trying to kill me, I knocked both off their feet again and tried to pull their guns away from them. It mostly worked, but bullets flew before I could subdue them.

Using my abilities, I propelled my body around them and blocked their escape, then knocked the rest of the guards off their feet.

The President raised his hands and faced me.

"I just want to have a conversation and show you something," I said, using my abilities to shut all the doors into the Oval Office. "Will you listen?"

"You've come a long way and caused a heck of a lot of damage for someone who wants to have a conversation," he replied as he straightened his suit.

"I know, but I'm a wanted criminal, and a bunch of people have gotten it into their heads that I'm extremely dangerous. They're not entirely wrong, but if I wanted you dead, you would be. Those plants would have throttled you instead of pinning you to your seat, so I had time to get through your Secret Service."

He studied me for a moment, and I let the other four men in the room get up. One of them found a gun and pointed it at me.

"It's all right, Clint," the President said, waving at the man to lower the weapon. "She's right. If she wanted to kill me, I'd be dead."

"Thank you," I replied.

"Well, I've agreed to hear what you have to say, but I won't promise to grant you anything when I'm done listening."

"That's fine. I just want you to listen, but I should let you know that you're not the only one. I'm carrying a body cam."

The President's eyebrows twitched. He motioned to the sofas to one side.

"Shall we sit? Do I need to let your dragon in? Or that other creature you often have? I understand they need to be close."

I followed him to the two sofas, and while he sat down on the end of one, I sat on the other. A moment later, Sen appeared, having wriggled through one of the gaps I'd made for the plant. She bounded onto my lap.

"Zephyr is too big to come inside," I said. "He's on your lawn, and he'll make sure we're not disturbed. But this is Sen. She's a myconid, a species of dryad."

"Nice to meet you," he said. "Now, please, tell me what you risked all this for." He motioned to the chaos and mess in his office. I'd blown papers and small ornaments off his desk, a vase was broken, and several pieces of furniture had been moved.

I focused on him. "I think you're aware that there was an agency tasked with keeping mythicals out of the public spotlight."

"Yes. It is my understanding that they used to relocate them until you came along and blew the whistle. So to speak."

"Are you also aware that your agency tried to kill me several times before I did so?"

"Is that why you're here?" he asked, frowning.

"Not exactly. Consider it background information." I pulled out my phone and played some footage from the battle where we'd publicly invited the world and the major news companies, and then Knox had attacked. It was a thirty-second clip.

"This was supposed to be where that agency ended. I demanded they leave us alone, and when they refused, we fought until they surrendered. I might have also wrecked the office they used."

The President smirked.

"I understand an agent died that day," he continued, looking more serious.

"Yes. A man called Knox. We tried to apprehend him alive and turn him over to be dealt with. I wasn't there when he died. I'd gone to follow some other agents and ensure they were prevented from harming any more mythicals. When I found Knox's superior, an agent called Crawley, she was talking to the head of the agency. He commanded her to kill me while I was there."

"Don't get me wrong, I'm sure this is important to you, but I'm still not sure where this is going," the President said, leaning to one side and resting his elbow on the arm of the sofa.

"Her superior. Jacobs. He reports directly to you, doesn't he?"

"Yes. And he's a—"

"You don't want to finish that sentence, Mr. President. Not until you've heard this." I pulled the recorder out of my pocket.

"We had a chat a little over twenty-four hours ago, and this is what he had to say for himself."

I pressed play and watched the President as he listened. I didn't ask if he recognized Jacobs' voice, but I'd called the agency's commander by name several times, and he hadn't denied it.

The President's face remained impassive while we

listened, but even he blanched when Jacobs admitted he wanted every last mythical dead and that I'd been framed for killing people.

Finally, silence filled the Oval Office. The four Secret Service agents were still standing close by. All of us looked at the man with the power.

"You say you acquired this only a short while ago?"

I nodded and took another deep breath, my heart pounding. "I let his men capture me once I'd worked out where he was. I persuaded his men to take me to him. This conversation happened then."

"That's not what he told me."

"I don't doubt that," I replied. "But that was his voice, those were his words, and now the whole world knows it. He didn't deny who he was. Didn't try to tell me I was wrong about him."

"No, that was him. And I believe you on that…"

"But now you don't know what to think," I finished for the President as his voice trailed off.

He looked at me again and studied my face, leaning forward.

"I have some questions for you if you'll answer them."

"Of course. I even swear to answer them truthfully."

"Right. How do you feel about the men you did kill? You don't seem to be remorseful."

"On the tape, I wasn't. As I said, I didn't think Jacobs would tell me how many died at my hands or the teams with me just for my own conscience, but he believed me to be a monster who only loved power, so I implied that was why I wanted to know. In truth, I wish no one had died."

"That doesn't entirely answer my question. How do you feel about the deaths?"

"I feel many things. Sometimes I'm glad someone on the agency side of things died. We've lost many mythicals. It feels like payback. But the majority of the time, I feel sad. Sick, even. If Jacobs hadn't been in charge of the agency, none of them would have died. No one on either side."

"You appear to be trying not to kill anyone. At least recently."

"I've always tried not to kill anyone. I've just got better at it with practice," I shot back. "There's been a lot of media pressure, but even when I did everything I could to not kill Jacobs faked it anyway."

"That must have made you angry."

"Of course. It would make anyone angry, but not enough for me to deliberately kill anyone. Again, if that was what I wanted, you'd be dead."

"So, what do you want?"

"Jacobs has to answer for what he's done. For the truth to be made public, and for a chance to show mythicals as they truly are. Peaceful, nature-loving, and phenomenal allies—and American citizens."

"They need to answer to someone. There needs to be oversight. You've broken the law."

"Yes, I have. I felt it was necessary, but I'll answer for those crimes if I can be kept safe and you guarantee I get a fair trial. The last time I submitted myself to the justice system, someone tried to blow me up."

"I'll point out that it's believed you'd blown yourselves up accidentally while trying to blow up others, but I have a feeling you'd tell me that was what Jacobs wants me to believe."

"Blowing things up isn't my style," I replied. "I'm an air and earth elf. I can do plenty of damage without fire and explosions."

The President nodded, and it felt as if our interview was coming to an end. But I'd done what I hoped to, and he'd listened. It also sounded as if he believed me.

"I'm willing to let myself be arrested now and go with Zephyr and Sen somewhere to be housed until something else can be sorted out. A trial, or whatever is considered necessary. I'm also happy to repair the damage to your wall. I do have one small request to make, however."

"You'd best spit it out," he replied as we all stood.

While I reached out with my powers and pulled the plants back outside, I looked at the President. Sen jumped up on my shoulder and held onto my hair.

"If you want to have someone report to you on the mythicals and help you to police them properly, I recommend my Shishou, an American citizen by the name of Minsheng. He's a good man. Part dwarf but mostly human. They trust him, but he's been in this country his whole life. A solid businessman and a good American. I'd recommend you talk to him about it if you don't use me."

"I'll bear that in mind. I'd want to see a résumé."

"He'll make sure you get it." As I spoke the last word, I closed the gap and made the wall look as good as new. Looking at the Secret Service agent, I nodded and lifted my hands to be handcuffed.

Before I knew what was happening, the President was shaking one of my hands.

"Thank you for coming to me with this, and for trusting me with the information," he said.

"Thank you for listening," I replied as the Secret Service ushered me away.

Zephyr's gas lingered in the hallway so I used my powers to blow it ahead of me and clear it out as more men and women came to escort me out. Zephyr fell in beside me and I reached for him, putting my hand on his scales. The agents spread out around us and continued to walk us away from the White House.

I still had my body cam rolling, but I needn't have bothered at this point. There were media cameras and helicopters everywhere and I didn't doubt that we were being broadcast on every channel in multiple countries. I'd just attacked the White House and walked away with everyone alive.

Now I had to trust the President would remove Jacobs from his job, if nothing else.

He will, Zephyr said. *And if not, you've just turned a bunch of people into supporters.*

I wasn't sure Zephyr was right, but waves of confidence rolled from him to me, and if nothing else, it helped me lift my head a little higher as I was tucked into the back of yet another police car.

CHAPTER TWENTY-FOUR

I exhaled with relief when Robert Johnson walked into the small room I was sitting in. There were no handcuffs on my wrists, and no one was officially keeping me here. Everyone knew it, so I'd been treated with respect. They'd also let Zephyr wait outside the building.

We'd been fed, offered drinks, and no one had been even slightly rude. But equally, I'd been given no information on what was happening outside the police station since I'd been brought there.

I'd refused to do anything or give any kind of statement until I'd seen a lawyer. The organization had come through for me again.

"Hello again, Aella," he said, giving me a nod before sitting down opposite me.

"I assume the organization agreed to pay for you again," I replied.

He nodded and put his briefcase on the table, then pulled out paper, a pen, and the familiar recorder he'd used the last time.

"They did. It will be my job to make sure you don't go to jail for anything after all this. Now, like last time, do you think you can tell me everything that happened in your words," he said as he sat down.

"I can, but first, could you answer a few questions? I've heard nothing. I need to know if everyone else is okay. If the Sanctuary is okay."

At first, my lawyer looked as if he might object to my questions, but eventually he relaxed and sat back in the metal chair.

"I can't speak to the latter, as I've had no information from them directly, but Minsheng, your Shishou, I believe, has been asked to see the President, and as far as I'm aware, he went. They must have talked over the mythical situation. Jacobs—I believe that's the man you mentioned in your broadcast—has been relieved of his job and is under investigation."

I exhaled with relief. I'd done it. Whatever followed next, I'd had Jacobs pulled out of the agency. It didn't mean the rest of the agents would be happy or start treating mythicals with respect overnight, but it gave me some hope that things would improve.

"And public opinion?" I asked.

"It's still mixed. Some people are always frightened of anything different, but you've certainly won over what I'd call the 'rational' element of America." Robert smiled as he spoke, and I felt another weight fall off my shoulders. If I'd begun to turn the tide and stopped the smear campaign, I had a chance to change things for the better.

With my worries allayed, I focused on the question my

lawyer had asked me. It was time to tell him what I'd been thinking and what had happened over the last few days.

It felt like it took an age, and I had to drink several cups of water, but eventually, I was done. Robert sat back once more and looked at me.

"I still can't quite believe everything that you're capable of," he said. "Or Zephyr and Sen."

Part of me wanted to grin and feel smug, but I was determined not to betray my emotions. I hadn't told Robert that Zephyr could now take human form. Thankfully, we didn't need to mention it, given Zephyr had been in dragon form for the entire attack on the White House.

Robert didn't ask me how Zephyr had helped get me out of the compound Jacobs had imprisoned me in, and I hadn't given much detail, focusing instead on how we'd tricked the agents and Jacobs into capturing me and taking me there.

"Well, so far they can charge you with treason for attacking the President, but in other respects, all they can really charge you with is assault and damage to government property. That said, there are a lot of counts, and it all adds up. Not to mention the way you fled after the explosion. There's now evidence to suggest that wasn't you, however."

"There is?" I asked, having almost forgotten about that after all the events that had followed.

"Yeah. Someone saw a person going up to that floor as all the agents and police left. They were carrying explosives, and a few witnesses came forward to say it looked as if everyone guarding you was in on it. All of the police officers involved in that night have been suspended pending an investigation, as well."

I exhaled. That hadn't been something I was expecting.

Ask him if we can press charges, Zephyr said into my head. *That explosion hurt, and it was meant to kill us.*

I passed on Zephyr's request, making it clear it was also something I wanted. The pain Zephyr had felt and what we'd had to put him through to flee in the subsequent days would take a long time to fade from my memory.

"Sadly, they've not caught anyone yet, but yes, if they did, we could push for attempted murder charges. It would depend on the evidence. I'll keep an eye on the progress of the case for you."

"Thank you," I replied. "For everything you're doing."

"Well, it's not over yet, but honestly, you did something incredibly brave to try to clear your name. I'm pretty sure the mythicals of the world owe you a huge amount of gratitude. I consider you a hero, and it's an honor to represent you." With this, Robert stood.

I moved to get up too, surprised he was leaving when we hadn't discussed strategy, but before either of us could do anything else, the sound of a key in the lock drew our attention, and a cop swung the door open.

Instead of coming in to say something, he pushed it wide open.

"Aella-Faye. You're free to go. The President has pardoned you of all crimes and insisted you be flown to him immediately."

I blinked, not sure how to react to what was being said.

It worked! Zephyr yelled, his delight breaking through

the shock. Sen did a happy little dance on my shoulder, and Robert fist-pumped the air.

"I'm free to go?" I asked. Of course, I could have walked out at any point, but the whole point of what I'd done and letting myself be arrested was to show that I would answer for crimes as any other mythical would.

"Yup. There's a chopper coming in to fetch you and take you to the White House. I've been told to make sure you're on it."

I nodded and walked toward the door, Robert motioning for me to go first. I was wearing an orange jumpsuit the prison had provided, but I'd only gone a little farther out of the room before someone handed me my clothes and pointed me in the direction of a changing room.

"Want me to wait around and make sure the exit process goes okay?" Robert asked.

I nodded automatically before going to get changed. Only once I was dressed in my own clothes, fingering a bullet hole in the edge of the jacket, did I begin to comprehend what was happening. It had all worked, and I was free to go back to my warehouse. The Sanctuary and all the mythicals we'd housed between us were safe.

It was almost too much of a relief to take, and by the time I was standing outside and leaning into Zephyr, tears of relief and gratitude were wetting my cheeks and dripping to the ground.

You did it, Zephyr said, nuzzling against me.

We did it, I replied. *None of it would have worked without you and Sen.*

Sen happy. The small myconid bounced up onto Zephyr.

Fly now?

I grinned as the chopper in the background landed, and a moment later, one of the pilots got out and came our way.

"Aella-Faye?" he asked as he came closer.

"Aella. I prefer just Aella." I said.

Robert gave my shoulder a squeeze before saying goodbye. I briefly wondered if I'd see him again. Although I admired the man and considered him an ally, a big part of me hoped not. I wanted this chapter of my life where I was never quite on the right side of the law to be over.

"Can you come with us, please?" the man asked, snapping me back to the present.

"Sure," I replied. "As long as I don't have to fly in the chopper with you. Zephyr and I are capable of getting anywhere we need, and I prefer to fly with him. I promise we'll follow you, though."

For a moment it looked as if he might object, but Zephyr stepped closer and lowered his head to nuzzle mine. The co-pilot took one look at the dragon and decided not to argue with us.

Grinning, I pushed air out with my hands and propelled myself and Sen onto Zephyr's back. It felt good to be in the open air again after being cooped up in the small police station's interrogation room for most of the night.

If I hadn't slept the day before I would have been exhausted, but I felt alive as Zephyr unfurled his wings and lifted all three of us into the air. We started flying in circles as the helicopter rose from the launch pad and joined us in the sky.

I motioned for the pilot to lead the way and Zephyr hung back, dropping down a little and coming alongside the craft so we could be seen by the co-pilot and they'd know we were keeping our promise.

I took control of the air around us, forming and shaping it to reduce the air resistance as Zephyr glided. At the chopper's speed it wasn't necessary, but I wanted the practice, and it gave me something to do.

As we'd been informed, we were led right back to the White House, our journey taking almost half as long again as it would have done had we been flying at Zephyr's top speed. In a way, it was amusing that they'd sent an aircraft to pick us up, but I had a feeling it was something to do with the ceremony of the moment.

News reporters noticed us coming, and we found ourselves almost surrounded by news helicopters getting images of us as we flew toward the large lawn in front of the building. There were more journalists on it, some with video camera crews and others with digital cameras around their necks or in one hand while they held microphones in the other.

I ignored them all, not sure what I'd say to any of them, anyway. Neither "Sorry I made you think I was going to kill the President," or, "Don't worry, I haven't come back to wreck the place a second time" seemed to be good options.

We could try the last one, Zephyr said, which made me chuckle.

Wrecking it or promising not to? I asked.

Either. Although the first would not be good since it is likely to get us arrested again.

So not that one, then?

No. They don't have good pizza in prison.

I laughed as Zephyr landed and I slid off his back to stand beside him. Camera flashes caught me off guard, making me blink. A million questions blurred into one mass of noise, then someone stepped forward, the familiar uniform of a Secret Service agent giving me a focal point.

"Aella-Faye, the President would like to see you in his office," the man said.

I recognized him as one of the men who'd escorted us out of the building the night before and had to fight back the smirk I wanted to give him. Bet he hadn't expected we'd be back so soon.

We were led across the lawn and away from all the reporters outside the gates, and I instantly felt better. I wasn't ready to answer any questions.

The door had already been replaced, but I noticed that it still smelled faintly of varnish as if it had been rushed through production. I only noticed it for a moment, however.

On the other side of the door were Minsheng, Daisy, and Chris. All of them were smiling, and Daisy rushed over and hugged me, narrowly missing crushing Sen as the myconid pulled herself up to stand on my shoulder.

For a moment, I knew nothing but the three of them and my relief at seeing they were okay and also free.

I hugged Minsheng last, my Shishou not letting go of me as quickly as the others had.

"You did it, Aella. You, Zephyr, and Sen made it work," he whispered before he let me go.

I smiled at him, but then the President appeared from his office.

"Good. You look well. I did insist they were kind to you until I got to the bottom of everything," the white-haired man said, his hand outstretched for me to head to the Oval Office.

I glanced at Zephyr, who was still standing outside with his head poking through the front door.

"I'd offer to talk somewhere your dragon friend could join us since he doesn't fit inside, but I don't want anyone to overhear what we have to say and report on it before I've done a press conference."

I'll be okay out here, Zephyr said. *I think it's best we keep my shapeshifting abilities to ourselves a little longer. At least, until we've heard what he has to say for himself.*

I agreed and followed the President with only Sen for company, noticing none of the others joined us, either.

"Please, sit down and let me tell you what's happened," the President said as he closed the Oval Office door. I noticed there were six Secret Service agents in the room with us, but they were all standing against the walls and staring at nothing.

"I've heard some of it," I replied, deciding not to be passive in this conversation. After all, the last time I was here, I'd pretty much demanded that I be heard and respected.

"Of course, I'm sure your lawyer will have told you what he could. I understand he was one of the first who was willing to represent your kind. I've sent him a message to thank him."

I lifted an eyebrow at this declaration but didn't interrupt. Whatever the President wanted to say, I was hoping he'd get to it.

"I've spent the night reviewing all the information I could get my hands on and the signed confession from Jacobs, the man in charge of the agency responsible for mythicals."

"He confessed?"

"Yes. After I had the recording you played me shown to him, he told me everything he'd done and why. Of course, he still believes he did the right thing, but thankfully, it's not up to him."

"And it is up to you?" I asked, trying to get him to the point a little quicker.

"Yes. I'm officially declaring all mythicals born in the United States to be American citizens and granted all rights. I'm also willing to sign a treaty with this sanctuary Minsheng has been telling me about. I believe we can recognize the land as theirs in a similar way we do the Native Americans tribal lands."

I nodded, stunned for a moment. That was more than I'd expected.

"I've also dismantled the agency. At least, the majority of it. I do feel there needs to be some oversight of the mythicals, as you call them, but Minsheng informs me that the Sanctuary already has a council to handle legal matters. He also tells me the mythicals report to you."

"They do. I'm considered a leader among many of them for my ability to use more than one element and bond with more than one mythical creature."

The President nodded, looking thoughtful. "In that case, I would like to ask you to work with a new agency tasked with helping to smooth over matters of justice and see that mythicals are policed fairly. Someone needs to be making sure these extra powers aren't used for the wrong reasons."

"I'd be willing to do that. Would you consider Agent Crawley? She was fired from the original agency for taking pity on me, and it turns out she has a half-elven daughter. She's shown she's dedicated to the US, but she has compassion for mythicals," I replied, suddenly thinking of her.

"She sounds perfect. I can't promise, but if all that's true, she'd definitely be a good place to begin."

"I understand that Zephyr, Sen, and I have been pardoned."

"You and all mythicals who were simply trying to defend themselves from the hatred Jacobs spread through the agency. I won't see any more of you hunted for the wrong reasons."

"Good." I got to my feet, feeling as if the meeting was done. There were still a few details to be worked out, but the mythicals in the country were no longer in danger, and I wasn't a wanted criminal anymore. Of all the outcomes, it was the best I could have hoped for.

"I have one last request from you before you return to LA," the President said as he got to his feet as well. "I'd like to do a joint press conference. With Zephyr there, as well."

Without hesitation, I smiled. I was more than happy. I was about to go on air with the President and publicly receive his endorsement. If that didn't help the American people like us, nothing would.

Reaching for Zephyr with my mind, I gave him a mental high five. We'd done it. Our kind were free, and so were we.

EPILOGUE

I exhaled as I sat down on my own bed.

We were back home after several days of traveling from the East Coast, and I was exhausted. We'd flown most of the way to the warehouse, stopping off and enjoying our newfound freedom and checking in with everyone else. They'd all come back in the large tour bus, and then they'd gone ahead of us with anyone who wanted to be in the warehouse for the foreseeable future.

In the days since our pardon, we'd been at the Sanctuary helping to set up the first liaison between the council and the human world to discuss laws and the treaty that would protect the land the Sanctuary was currently on for generations to come.

While not everyone on the council had been thrilled at the idea of having a human come to the Sanctuary, their reception had been far warmer than ever before, and I'd had a much-needed lesson with the elven masters.

All four had wanted to train me, the fire and water masters determined to see which of the two remaining elements I would show an aptitude for next. Eventually, I'd excused myself, and Zephyr had flown us back home.

Of course, then I'd had to talk to everyone who had stayed behind and everyone who had come back two days before us and tell them everything, despite most of them knowing it all.

Finally, they'd let me leave, and I'd climbed the stairs to the bedroom I shared with Sen and Zephyr.

Zephyr was still in dragon form, but he rested himself on the bed anyway, the room having been designed to account for a full-grown dragon.

I was about to suggest we got some sleep or went up to the roof to watch the sunrise when there was a gentle tap at the door. Erlan opened it, a laptop in his hands, his eyes wide.

"Is now a good time?" he asked, his voice barely above a whisper.

If it had been anyone else, I'd have said no, but Erlan's eyes were wide, and he glanced over his shoulder more than once. Something was clearly bothering him, and he didn't want the others to know about it.

"I think it will need to be," I replied, waving him into the room.

He shut the door behind him and brought the laptop over to me.

"After we got back, I decided it would be a good idea to keep track of all the information we've gathered and keep track of how many copies and who had access to it. Some of it is sensitive stuff, after all," Erlan said.

"Like the lab information from the elves the agency

experimented on?" I replied, getting a bad feeling in my gut. At the same time, Zephyr lifted his head off the bed.

"Yes, that and what you're capable of. Who lives here. Everything we have. I found something I don't understand."

I exhaled and bit down on the words I wanted to reply. If Erlan didn't understand something to do with the computer, that wasn't a good sign.

"I'm pretty sure someone has been transferring copies of everything to a secure server somewhere else. One that's masked and rerouted and all sorts of complicated things."

"Someone?" I asked, beginning to feel sick, understanding just enough to know Erlan was telling me something serious.

"A person in the warehouse. The origin is almost always the warehouse. I traced the data as far as I could, but I only managed to glean one piece of information about the server it was sent to and the location."

Erlan turned the laptop around to show me a strange symbol on a company webpage.

"This was on the dark web for that IP."

"What is it?" I asked, having a feeling I should know from the way he was looking at me.

"Has anyone at the Sanctuary mentioned a sect of mythicals who broke off from the organization and Sanctuary after the prophecy of your coming?"

I nodded, my heart beginning to pound.

"This is their symbol. It's banned in the Sanctuary, and for good reason."

"Because they're the ones who want to reopen the

magical portals," I replied, shuddering as I repeated words one of the elven masters had spoken months earlier.

"Yes. They want to bring more mythicals to Earth, and they don't necessarily want or care if humanity survives that encounter."

"They're everything Jacobs feared the mythicals would become," I said, my gaze meeting Erlan's as I reached for Zephyr with a hand, desperate for some comfort.

"Exactly. And someone in the warehouse has been telling them everything."

WATER BOUND

The story continues with *Water Bound*, book 7 in the Dragon of Shadow and Air series.

Claim your copy today!

ACKNOWLEDGMENTS

A huge huge thank you to LMBPN and everyone who works there for everything you do with me and these books. You all rock, especially the editing team for putting up with my Britishisms and fixing all my errors.

To Bear and David for all the plot help, yet again. You guys are the best.

To my tiny humans for being little rays of sunshine when I need it most, even if I'd get far more work done if you weren't asking me for yet another snack.

And to my friends, for supporting me and understanding me even when I'm not sure what I am trying to do or why yet.

To my readers for all the encouraging messages you keep sending me. They keep me getting up each day and they keep me writing. Without you this career wouldn't be anywhere near so magical.

Finally, to God, for knowing how to catch someone when the fall. Every time.

ABOUT THE AUTHOR

Jess was born in the quaint village of Woodbridge in the UK, has spent some of her childhood in the States and now resides near the beautiful Roman city of Bath. She lives with her husband, Phil, her two tiny humans (one boy and one girl) and her very dapsy cat, Pleaides.

During her still relatively short life Jess has displayed an innate curiosity for learning new things and has therefore studied many subjects, from maths and the sciences, to history and drama. Jess now works full time as a writer and mummy, incorporating many of the subjects she has an interest in within her plots and characters.

When she's not busy with work and keeping her tiny humans alive she can often be found with friends, playing with miniature characters, dice and pieces of paper covered in funny stats and notes about fictional adventures her figures have been on.

You can find out more about the author and her upcoming projects by joining her on facebook, by watching her live D&D streams, or emailing her via books@jessmountifield.co.uk. Jess loves hearing from a happy fan so please do get in touch!

Jess is also opening up her discord for fans to come chat about what she's up to, and see a few sneak peaks of future work. There's also a chance to become one of her beta readers. If you'd like to check that out you can do so here.

CONNECT WITH JESS

Connect with Jess Mountifield

Mailing list sign up
Facebook group.
Discord group
Actual play D&D stream: Twitch or Youtube
Email address: contact me here.

BOOKS BY JESS MOUNTIFIELD

Already published
Urban Fantasy
Dragon of Shadow and Air:
Air Bound (Book 1)
Shadow Sworn (Book 2)
Dragon Souled (Book 3)
Earth Bound (Book 4)
Night Sworn (Book 5)
Dryad Souled (Book 6)
Water Bound (Book 7)

Fantasy
Tales of Ethanar:
Wandering to Belong (Tale 1)
Innocent Hearts (Tale 2 & 3)
For Such a Time as This (Tale 4)
A Fire's Sacrifice (Tale 5)

Winter Series:
The Hope of Winter (Tale 6.05)
The Fire of Winter (Tale 6.1)

Guild of the Eternal Flame:

Wayfarer's Sanctuary

Protector's Secret

Healer's Oath

Other Fantasy:

The Initiate (under Holly Lujah)

Writing with Dawn Chapman:

Jessica's Challenge (#5 in the Puatera Online series)

Dahlia's Shadow (#6 in the Puatera Online series)

Lila's Revenge (#7 in the Puatera Online series)

Sci-Fi:

Fringe Colonies:

Alliance

Haven

Rebellion

Rebirth

Reclamation

Star Trail:

Hunted

Sherdan series:

Sherdan's Prophecy

Sherdan's Legacy

Sherdan's Country

Sherdan's Road (A short story in the anthology 'The End of the

Road')

The Slave Who'd Never Been Kissed (A short in the charity anthology 'Imaginings')

New Beginnings

Santa's Little Space Pirate

In the multi-author Adamanta series:

Episode 1 – Adamanta

Episode 3 – Excelsior

Episode 8 – Phoenix

Episode 13 – New Contacts

Episode 17 – Sacrifice

Other:

Clues, Claws and Christmas

Non-Fic:

How to Write Lots, and Get Sh*t Done: the Art of Not Being a Flake

Find purchase links here

Coming soon:

Urban Fantasy:

Dragon of Shadow and Air:

Water Bound

Day Sworn

Fantasy

(Tales of Ethanar):

The Pursuit of Winter (#2 in the Winter series, Tale 6.2)

Books under Amelia Price

Mycroft Holmes Adventures:

The Hundred Year Wait

The Unexpected Coincidence

The Invisible Amateur

The Female Charm

The Reluctant Knight

The Ambitious Orphan

The Unconventional Honeymoon Gift

The Family Reunion

The Immortal Problem

Coming soon:

The Unremarkable Assistant

OTHER BOOKS FROM LMBPN
PUBLISHING

Sign up for the LMBPN email list to be notified of new releases and special deals!

https://lmbpn.com/email/

For a complete list of books by LMBPN please visit:

https://lmbpn.com/books-by-lmbpn-publishing/

www.ingramcontent.com/pod-product-compliance
Lightning Source LLC
LaVergne TN
LVHW041625060526
838200LV00040B/1434